BEiNG HUMAN

— A NOVEL BY —

CHRISTINA GRANT

Karl —
I look forward to reading
your book someday too!

Christina

BEING HUMAN

Copyright © 2015 Christina Grant

ISBN: 0994029217
ISBN-13: 978-0994029218

Jacket design, text design and typsestting: Kathy Grant

TO MARY SHELLEY, the Mother of Science Fiction, and to all the writers of Sci-Fi and Fantasy who followed her, who have created all worlds, both the possible and impossible.

/ CONTENTS

1 / ACCOUNT ON A MIRACLE

Once upon a time, there was a piece of wood.
– Carlo Collodi, *The Adventures of Pinocchio*

YOU'VE ASKED ME to write about how I began: How do I feel – or do I feel anything at all. Write it down for the record, you told me. For the future. You've seen the news on Intelli!net—my story is not wholly new. Yet, who better to chronicle my strange, slow birth than me?

Once upon a time, there was a jumble of circuitry, a mound of metal, plastic, and ceramic bits…

Oh, but it's hard to tell a story from the beginning when you're not sure where the beginning is. Human memory is erratic at best. My memories are no longer stored in neat compartments, waiting until my electronic mind requests a specific fact. Cells no longer regenerate, synapses fire randomly. Memories link themselves to smells, to faces, to locations. One memory begets another. Others fade into an inaccessible past.

My memories are layered, not like the layers of an onion, but like a slice of frosted layer cake. You can see what happened in the beginning, middle, later. They fit sequentially together when observing them objectively, but when you try to extract a layer—get into the middle of it—everything just gives way under pressure and the layers melt together, a jumble of flavours and images and sounds, and I'm not sure what happened first or what will happen next. I'm not sure of anything at all anymore. Here is what I know: I was made. I was awakened. I was.

Then along came Bean.

I have been asked over the years to explain what being a robot feels like. It doesn't feel like anything. There was no "I"; merely an awareness of function. I had no choice of whether or not to comply. I had no concept of wanting anything. I was as reliant on my programming as a worker ant on her instinct.

As my self-awareness programming slowly developed, I began to feel myself, first like a television program running in the background; you are aware of it but not giving it your full attention. Later, the feeling floated up to my consciousness, the way you notice an itch on your leg for the first time.

It's hard to determine exactly when my humanity took form. Outwardly, it all began with five fingers on an open palm. The miracle began as modern-day miracles often do: with an experiment.

Sometimes my memories bubble up in dreams like cargo from a sunken ship. Bits and pieces of seemingly random objects and events float on my consciousness: brightly coloured silks fanning in the breeze, a fat teddy bear, a shelf crammed with books, a wooded park, a single eye. If I were more machine than I am now, I might have been able to list exact events with perfect recall. My memory is no longer flawlessly linear. But if I were less of the man that I am now, an error message might have popped up: Access denied: cannot find file source. How would I make sense of any of this? I am less, yet I am more.

First memories often consist of the people closest to you: Your mother singing to you the same series of bedtime songs each night as you drift off to sleep; a family dog, which at the time seemed the biggest, softest thing in the room upon which to rest your head; your best friend in the neighbourhood who, after a small argument, dumped a bucket of water over your head.

My first memory was of someone shining a light into my eyes. Everything around me was dark except for that blinding pinpoint of light. I like to imagine that true newborns have a similar experience, only bloodier and blindingly abrupt.

"It's functional," a voice spoke, floating somewhere just beyond the light.

"Registering visual and auditory input," the voice continued. "Signs normal. Processor functioning at normal parameters." It was not exactly your typical bedtime lullaby, sung by one whose arms enfold you securely as you drift off to sleep.

What seemed like an instant later—although according to my internal clock it was weeks later—I was booted up in my recharging dock housed inside a small, person-sized closet. I was completely enclosed since people found it disconcerting to see one of us plugged in and unconscious. The door opened, and a female face, angular and symmetrical, appeared. Behind her peeked out a smaller face, soft and round and surrounded with waves of deep red hair. The smaller face opened her mouth and stuck out her tongue. Her green eyes crossed as if trying to focus on something on the bridge of her nose.

My facial recognition program helped me to distinguish gender, age, and emotion from the complex mapping of human faces. By the slight lines around her thin mouth and the creases around her eyes, I estimated the woman to be in her late forties. I tracked the involuntary head movement caused by blood pumping to her brain. The slight elevation in pulse rate combined with a light blush, widened eyes, and slight frown indicated that she was feeling mildly apprehensive but interested.

The young girl was about ten years old. By her wide eyes and large smile, I concluded that she was feeling extremely curious and playful, not that I had any firsthand experience of any emotion; I was merely programmed to react in a prescribed manner according to the dominant mood of the people around me.

The woman squinted at my face, looked down at the small screen she held in her hand.

"SimAid activate," her voice went up like a question, as if she was unsure.

"SimAid activated," was my programmed response. "How may I be of assistance, Ma'am?"

2 / ACTIVATION

THE MISTRESS OF the household had ordered me a year ago. Despite the couple's high standing in the company, their order was placed in sequence on a waiting list. Of course, I was the newest model on the market--nothing but the best for Catherine Archambault. As your typical SimAid 3.3, I was programmed to do common housework, such as vacuuming, cleaning windows and floors, dusting, and tidying up. A glorified cyslave, really. My particular model was upgraded with the impression of companionship. I was able to nod in simulated sympathy to lengthy exchanges of verbal information, even if no response was required of me. I assembled my face into a frown if the person speaking with me frowned, and adopted the pre-programmed amiable expression if they smiled. My features and form had been designed to give the impression of pleasant submission without seeming too eerily human. In the age of customization and personalization, I was plainly made. My features and body were indicative of the male gender with wider shoulders and squared jaw. My face was free of any etched corporate designs, multicoloured stones, or bright alloy adornment. My body was metallic, humanoid, but not too realistic. People don't like to mistake their machines for themselves. However, we still needed to function within the structure of human buildings and we needed to use your tools. If thinking machines had not been created in human form, all modern architecture and invention would have had to change; so for practical reasons, we have been created in your form.

We had never been terribly good at the fine detail. Sure, you created intelligent machines to clean your houses, tell you when the milk in the fridge had gone sour, build and maintain your automobiles, or assemble the smallest nanobots. But we couldn't tell when your pet was ill by stroking its fur. We could not distinguish between a ripe and overripe avocado. We had never felt a pinprick chill change to warmth when a snowflake melted on our fingertips.

I first met Sabine as a child, she being the child, not me. I, of course, was a being made out of metal and ceramic and plastics. I was a kitchen gadget, a household appliance. Call me what you will.

She called me Alek.

I didn't see her much for the first several days. I caught glimpses of her heels as she ran to hide around corners. I heard giggles drifting from another room. A few times, I had to remove a pile of gifts from the recharging dock (one striped knee sock, a stuffed toy, a chocolate bar wrapper, a black chess piece)—the only evidence of her presence and her acknowledgement of mine.

"I'm Sabine," she said the first time I saw the whole of her. I had joined the household earlier that week, uploaded a floor plan of the house and connected with the main terminal to enable my communication with fridge, oven, Intelli!net, every Intelli!tech device in the house. We were a seamlessly running, well-oiled Intelli!home.

She sat in the kitchen on a high stool pulled up to the breakfast bar. Despite the beautiful table in the adjoining dining room, I rarely saw the three members of the Archambault family eat together. Instead, they came in at various points throughout the day and ate either directly out of the fridge or sat briefly at the tall breakfast bar in the kitchen. Bean's slim legs hung just under the long counter, swinging back and forth in time to something she was listening to through bright pink ear buds. She had pulled one out of her ear so she could talk to me; the bud dangled from its wire like a tiny embryo on its umbilical cord.

"My family calls me Bean, because when I was born I was so small. You can call me that."

"Yes, Miss," I said. One of the flaws of my particular model was that I was difficult to reprogram unless given specific instructions.

"No. Bean." Bean corrected, her voice slow and steady. "Call me Bean."

"Yes, Bean." My original programming prescribed that I call any child in the household Master or Miss and the adults by their title and surname. I had already been instructed to use Dr. Catherine and Dr. Sebastien, which saved any confusion of calling them both Dr. Archambault.

"Do you have a name?" Bean asked as she jumped down from the stool. She stood looking up at me with her arms crossed, her head tilted to the side, her brows furrowed.

"I am SimAid 3.3."

"That's not a name, that's a type," she huffed, dropping her arms at her sides. "It's like calling me Girl, 10.6 years. You need a name."

I stood silently, waiting for instruction. I wasn't prepared to give myself a name.

Bean stood back a bit and rocked on the heels of her bare feet. She then stood as tall as her diminutive stature would permit on pointed toes and leaned in towards me, staring at my face.

"Alek," she said finally. "Somehow, you look like an Alek." I registered the name. Alek.

"I will respond when called by the name of Alek," I acknowledged. Bean smiled in satisfaction and patted me on the arm.

"Let's play, Alek."

And so it was Bean and Alek, Alek and Bean.

I've read that some children have invisible friends. Others talk to their dolls or treat their pets as playmates. Bean had me, and I had Bean. She dressed me up in her mother's old clothes and told me elaborate stories of daring princesses who rescued knights from fiery dragons. She showed me how to lower onto my hands and knees so she could stand on my back to climb the pear trees in the backyard. She liked to play school and jail. I was either the student or the convict; both seemed to be similar roles. Either way, I had to sit quietly, do what Bean told me and purposefully act up every so often so that she could properly punish me. Play time with Bean was as intricately scripted as a

Stratford Festival Theatre performance. In the middle of play, Bean would stop acting out her particular role to direct me on what to say or do next.

Her parents had no idea that I had become Bean's playmate. They were busy and often out of the house. They thought it sensible to leave a precocious girl of not-quite-eleven by herself for hours on end. She was highly imaginative; she could amuse herself adequately. To them, I was still a SimAid. I greeted visitors and turned away salespeople. I cleaned. I answered the phone. I cooked. I shopped. When I was not needed, I retired to my charging closet.

Another of my duties was to pick up Bean from school at the end of the day. Bean had just started grade six the previous week at The Cummings School for the Gifted. I would walk with her the short distance home, crossing busy streets and crammed subdivisions until we reached the more luxuriously spread-out neighbourhood where her family lived.

Like many families in the area, Bean's parents worked in the fastest growing industry that the town had seen in decades: Technology And Robotics In Action, or TARIA, as it was referred to in the media and stock markets worldwide. All Intelli!technology, which now flooded the world, originated from minds at TARIA. In town, the company owned a large percentage of land upon which its various departmental buildings were housed. Many graduates from the local two major universities and three colleges were recruited into the business. TARIA sponsored several local sports complexes and theatre houses. The company was the town, and the town was the company.

It wasn't unusual for students to be carrying around the latest technological TARIA marvel, and in this case, Bean had me. By now, every wealthy household on the planet had a central Intelli!tech computer running the daily functioning of their house and a robotic servant to keep up with daily chores. I was the first domestic robot who was sufficiently advanced to leave the house and to be trusted to accompany a child home. Safety was no problem: I had GPS capabilities, access to the entire Intelli!net, and was honed in on Bean's Intelli!plant, which most children had by walking age. Their parents were able to track them with the small device implanted under the skin of the forearm just above the wrist.

It was late in the summer. If you asked a student, he or she would tell you it was already fall, because the nights were cooler and school had started up again. The first few times that I walked Bean to and from school, a crowd of children had followed us like I was the electronic Pied Piper. Children spoke to me, touched my arms. They obviously had older SimAid models in their own homes, but none as advanced as me. Bean's parents worked at a high level of robotics development and testing.

"Hey, what model is this SimAid?"

"Does it do your homework?"

"Do you think it could run as fast as my dog?

"Can it come over to my house and play with my SimAid?"

"He's Alek—a SimAid 3.3," Bean answered patiently. "He's not allowed to do my homework, but he can help. He can't go to your house. But you can come over if you want." She added quickly. I hadn't met any of Bean's friends. No one yet had visited her home. Suddenly, a small boy stepped forward. His freckles stood out in sharp contrast to his pale face.

"Hello, Alek," he said seriously, holding out his right hand. "My name is Russell."

Still walking, I looked down at the boy's proffered appendage. Bean giggled.

"You shake it," she whispered in the direction of my auditory receptors. I held out my hand in front of me and shook it up and down in the air. Bursts of laughter erupted from the children around me.

"No," said Russell, grabbing my hand, "like this." We stopped walking as he grasped my hand more firmly than I would have expected from one with such skinny arms, and pumped up and down a few times. He let go of my hand. As we began walking again, the crowd of children followed us still.

"Does he sing?"

"Can he tell stories?"

"Is he allowed to babysit me when my parents are away?"

"Will he come to your recitals?"

Bean stopped walking. I stopped with her.

"I suppose . . . if he wants to hear me play." She started walking again. I kept up beside her.

"What do you play?" I asked her. A chorus of whispers swept around us like a sudden gust of wind. Older SimAid models were not programmed to speak unless spoken to and didn't ask questions except for clarification of tasks. The bright smile on Bean's face expressed delight at my programmed curiosity.

"I play the cello."

"Cello. A large stringed instrument of the violin family that is held upright between a seated player's knees and played with a bow."

Like all Intelli!bots, I had instant and continuous access to all information available through Intelli!net: unlimited knowledge.

"Yes. I just started playing last year at school. I really want private lessons, but my parents want me to focus on my school work."

"Why do you like playing the cello?"

When Bean stopped abruptly again, the small paparazzi of school children following closely behind nearly ran into us.

"Nobody's ever asked me that before."

"Not your parents?"

"No."

"Your friends?" Bean looked down at her feet. I could see her features turn down, frowning.

"Uh, no."

"Then why do you like playing the cello?"

"I . . . oh, I guess everything kind of fades around me. I forget where I am, how I feel. There's only the music, and I'm the one making it. But in a way, it's like the music's making me too, you know?"

I stood still, looking at her face for help in translating what she had just said. She must have realized I had trouble processing her answer; after a moment, she said, "It, uh, playing cello makes me happy, you know?"

I nodded my head up and down in automated empathy. I did not know.

3 / AMITY

It's your fiction that interests me. Your studies of the interplay of human motives and emotion.
– Isaac Asimov, *I, Robot*

ONE SATURDAY NIGHT, the Archambaults were invited to attend TARIA's Community Innovation Awards Gala. They decided to leave me at home to babysit Bean. Why pay for a sitter now that I was here, working for free? While I cooked up a small meal of pasta and sauce for Bean, Catherine readied herself upstairs in her voluminous bath and change room. Bean's father, Sebastien, sat at the high counter with Bean, his eyes flicking back and forth between his daughter and the Intelli!net news broadcast on the wall. The !screen showed extreme snowstorms hitting the eastern coast.

"—and then Mrs. Edgecomb froze like a statue and told Russell to pick up the pencil he threw, so he walked over and picked up the pencil, then dropped it again and said, 'There. I picked it up.' Mrs. Edgecomb's face got so red it was almost purple. Russell got in so much trouble and had to go down to the principal's office and call his parents, who were on holidays in the Canadian Republic of Turks and Caicos, so his nanny had to talk to the principal, and she doesn't speak anything but French." Bean took a breath. In the short pause, her dad turned to look at her.

"Russell, huh? Is he a friend of yours?"

"No, dad, he's just in my class. He plays the viola really well, though. The other day when Mr. Liu was conducting, Russ took a piece of gum he'd found under his seat and. . ." As she spoke again, her father's eyes drifted back to the wall. I placed a bowl of pasta in front of Bean.

"Thanks, Alek." She grinned at me. "You make the best pasta."

"Ditalini." I answered.

"Pardon?"

"The type of pasta is ditalini, meaning 'little thimble' in Italian, in reference to its shape."

"Huh." Bean spoke through the ditalini that she was already stuffing in her mouth.

Sebastien's eyes turned back from the Intelli!screen to his daughter.

"What did you call it?" His eyebrows raised. Bean swallowed before answering.

"Ditalini."

"No, I mean the SimAid."

"Oh! Alek. He likes it, don't you, Alek?"

"If it pleases Dr. Sebastien and Dr. Catherine."

"Alek," Sebastien spoke the name slowly. "Yes, that would be easier, wouldn't it? Why not?"

"What would be easier?" Bean's mother appeared in the doorway in a dazzle of jewelry at her ears, wrist, and throat. A thousand tiny beads in her dress caught the light and shimmered at her slightest movement. She stood with one foot slightly forward and angled out, a hand on her hip, as if waiting for something that I didn't quite understand.

Sebastien stood, smiling at his wife.

"Catherine, you look stunning."

"Thank you, Sebastien. Are we ready? Sabine, wipe your face on a napkin, please." Bean swiped at her face.

"Dad agrees that we can call him Alek," Bean said, patting my arm.

"But why?" Catherine frowned slightly.

"Because he needs a name."

"All right. Fine." Catherine waved her hand as if clearing the idea from the air.

"Shall we?" Bean's father held out his arm.

"Yes." Catherine's face relaxed as she took her husband's elbow.

"Adam has reserved us seats at his table. We'll be right down front when he gets his award."

"What award?" Bean asked.

"Oh, Adam Trent is receiving an award for innovation in home technology. He is the genius creator of SimAids, you know."

"Hey, Alek, I guess that makes him your dad!"

"Well, I wouldn't say—"

"Your dad's getting an award! Aren't you excited, Alek?" She jumped up and down.

"We won't be back until after midnight." Sebastien cut in,

turning to us as he helped Catherine with her coat. "Can you stay in working mode until then, uh, Alek?"

"I will not retire to my charging closet until your return."

"Great. Goodnight Lima Bean."

"Goodnight Daddy!" She jumped into her father's arms and squeezed him. "Goodnight Mother." Bean turned to hug her mother.

"Watch my dress, your hands are all full of sauce." Mrs. Archambault held Bean at arms' length looking at her as if noticing her for the first time, then gave her a small kiss on the forehead.

"Be good, love."

Bean waved goodbye from the front window until the car swooshed around the corner and out of sight. She then turned to me and said, "Whaddaya wanna play?"

"Pardon me?"

"What do you want to play?" she repeated, bouncing slightly on her heels.

"You will have to teach me some games. I have not been programmed to play."

Bean stopped bouncing for a moment then said, "Rock Star."

"How do you play Rock Star?"

"First we have to dress up." Bean grabbed my arm and pulled me towards the stairs. I climbed the stairs while Bean hopped two steps at a time into her room.

I could not say whether Bean's was a typical young girl's room since I had never seen any but hers. Her double bed was covered in a bright red comforter and strewn with pillows and the odd stuffed animal. Her cello stood against the corner of a wall beside a chair and a music stand. It was the only space that showed the carpet beneath. Outside of a large wedge of clean floor space surrounding the cello corner, the rest of Bean's room was an explosion of clothing and toys falling out of her half-opened closet. Her desk was covered in drawings, paper, and coloured pencils.

"Here's my journal," she said, taking a small notebook from the clutter of her desk. "I like writing with a pen and paper. I feel so old-fashioned. Like a girl from a real book."

"What do you write?"

"Just stuff. Things I notice. Things I like and don't like." She tossed the book back onto the pile and flung herself backwards on the bed.

Shelves lining one entire wall were filled with books and small items such as an old-fashioned wind-up music box, a cracked teacup, a fishbowl with half-evaporated water and algae-coated stones but no fish, and a bank shaped like a rabbit. Her wall was plastered in seemingly random photos and artwork: many fuzzy and wide-eyed baby animals, a grainy black and white photograph of a man standing on a moving motorcycle, a famous female cellist playing her instrument with her eyes closed, a drawing of a circle of laughing girls holding hands in a field, some obviously enhanced photos of several teenaged movie or music stars whom I'd seen on previews and promos, all with symmetrical faces and asymmetrical hair styles.

Bean noticed me taking in the gallery on her wall.

"That's Jenny Lee," she said, pointing to the cellist. "I want to play like her one day. And that's my great-great grandfather," she pointed to the man standing on the motorcycle. "He was an inventor and a daredevil. He flew airplanes in World War II. Can you believe that there was once a war that the whole world got involved in?" She pointed at one of the movie star photos.

"Have you ever seen Neil Marshall in any of his movies? He's SOOO talented!"

"I've never watched a movie."

"Then we'll watch one tonight! But after Rock Star." She disappeared into her large closet like a spelunker into a cave. I heard shuffling, scraping, and a small bang. A few moments later, Bean reappeared with an armful of clothing.

"I'll help you find a costume." She dropped the pile on top of another mound of clothing and started rifling through. Bean finally took out a large black leather jacket.

"Try this on." I pulled the jacket on. It was the first item of clothing I had worn. I turned to show Bean, who was already dressed over her pyjamas in an oversized bright blue dress with zippers going up the sides. She wobbled slightly in a pair of high, brown boots.

"Next, accessories." Bean pulled open a drawer in her desk. She took out a large chain and draped it around my neck. She looped a similar chain around herself, and added a few bangles to her wrists. She motioned me over to the mirror on her closet door.

"Come see."

I stared at our reflection. I definitely did not see two rock stars. I saw a humanoid robot in a jacket and a young girl dressed in too-large adult clothing.

"I may be lacking sufficient imagination."

"Forget about it." Bean shoved aside some pencils on her desk and grabbed an Intelli!pad. "Now we need music. How about Not Penny's Boat?" She tapped the screen in a few places and the music started up, slow and quiet.

"Why are they called Not Penny's Boat?"

"My parents told me it's a reference to some show called Lost they used to watch. It was on way before I was born. Episodes are on Intelli!net now, of course, but I'm not allowed to watch it until I'm older. You used to only be able to watch certain shows at specific times. People were glued to their TVs, dad said. I don't understand why they wouldn't let people watch their shows anytime, anywhere. Who tells you when you're allowed to read a book?" She took a breath as Not Penny's Boat began to sing.

"Here, you play drums. Like this." Bean handed me a pair of pencils after miming a drumming demonstration. "I'll play guitar and sing vocals."

She grabbed the music stand and pulled it as high as it would go. She began mouthing the words of the music into the top of the stand, her eyes squeezed shut, an expression of physical pain on her face. Every so often, she stopped and strummed the invisible guitar strung around her chest. Her hair whipped around with the faster parts of the song. I obediently drummed my imaginary drums and tried to mimic Bean's expression of anger and agony. She stopped suddenly.

"What are you doing with your face?"

"I'm attempting to imitate your expressions." The latest SimAid face plates were made up of several layers of moveable parts—eyebrows, mouth, cheeks—so that we could mimic human expressions and thereby increase feelings of empathy towards us.

"Well don't. You can't do it right. It looks silly."

We played four or five songs, each one sounding similar to the last. I didn't understand yet how music affected the human consciousness. It was all rhythm and riffs and blended harmonies. I could almost see the music unfold in metered uniformity, but I didn't feel the emotion behind it.

Finally, sweaty and out of breath, Bean tapped the Intelli!pad and the music stopped.

"What do you want to do now?" she asked.

"May I hear you play the cello?" I asked, accessing my polite social interaction programming. People loved to share their skills.

Bean stepped out of her dress and kicked off her boots, which went flying back into the depths of the cavernous closet. She grabbed the music stand, lowered it into place, the rested her Intelli!pad on it. Bean gingerly picked up her cello and bow and sat down in front of the music stand. She tapped the !pad to find a piece of music.

"Sit down," she motioned to her bed with her bow. I sat on the edge of her red comforter.

Bean's right hand hovered, holding her bow in a relaxed grip over the strings. She began pulling the bow back and forth across the strings as her left hand pressed different spots along the neck of the instrument. A long, slow sound started from its depths. Another note was added. As I listened, I realized that the song was the one we had first sung by Not Penny's Boat. It didn't sound quite the same; it was not as textured, the beat was imagined, and it was slower. But the melody was present, solitary and pure, in some way. I couldn't quite describe it then.

How does a machine explain music?

The song ended, and Bean closed her eyes. The final note hung in the air for a moment like a humming bird, then just as quickly disappeared.

I clapped. My hands made muffled clunking sounds, not at all like the sounds of living palms striking warmly together. My applause sounded like a pair of plastic serving spoons colliding. Bean opened her eyes and smiled.

"Thank-you."

"You played well. Where did you find the music to that song?"

"I arranged it myself." Even I knew that was a difficult and rare feat for an eleven-year old.

"Very well done."

Bean smiled again and placed her cello and bow in the corner. She shut off the Intelli!pad and placed it on her desk, announcing, "Snack time."

An hour later, after a snack of peanut butter and apples and a quick game of chess, Bean brushed her teeth and climbed under her covers. I stood beside the bed, watching her arrange blankets around her small body.

"Thank you, Alek. I had fun with you tonight." She sat up and wrapped her arms around me, squeezing tightly.

"Goodnight." I had heard her mother and father say it before leaving her room at night. When she finally released me, I walked out of the room, closing the door behind me.

At the time, I felt nothing.

Some days when I went to pick up Bean from school, I arrived early and would wait. Bean had strings ensemble every day last period, so I stood along the wall at the back of the room with the other children's nannies. The first few times I arrived, I caused a spectacle, being the only robotic babysitter in existence. The children stopped playing and stared. Their teacher, Mr. Liu, was a small, energetic man who used humour to motivate the children and keep them focussed. Bean and her classmates loved him, and she often told me stories about him.

Today when all the children turned around to stare at me, Mr. Liu spoke above the whispers.

"Yes, it's terribly exciting to have a virtual nanny in the classroom. You can ask Sabine later if she's found his emergency sleep switch so she can sneak junk food and stay up late when her parents are away," the teacher said, winking. The students laughed, then set their bows to their instruments and went back to playing.

One spring day when I arrived to pick up Bean, another teacher stood in Mr. Liu's place at the front of the room behind the tall music stand. She was as different from the former teacher as anyone could be. Where Mr. Liu was short and portly, Miss Graham was tall and weedy.

"She's awful, I hate her!" Bean announced the moment we had left the building.

"Who?" I asked her. Sometimes I had difficulty following human train of thought. It seemed to jump around quite a bit.

"Miss Graham. She scowls and yells at us all the time. She's like a blonde, frizzy-haired witch! Did you see that bruise on her neck? I swear she spends her free time in the broom closet with

Mr. Charles, the custodian."

"I thought that bruising under the chin occurs with violinists since the chin rest puts pressure on the capillaries of the neck. Isn't that why the students who play violin and viola have sponges affixed with elastics around their chin rests?"

"Don't ruin a good story," she huffed.

"Do you mean to say that your accounts are fictional?"

"Yes, it's just something that all the kids say."

"But why do you spread false events as if they are real?"

"I guess because sometimes a story is so much more interesting than the truth."

I struggled to comprehend the logic.

Over the next few weeks, Miss Graham was a frequent topic of conversation on the walk home from school. On this particular day, Bean seemed to relish the latest emotional injury inflicted by her teacher.

"Do you know what happened today? Russell secretly brought his pet iguana, Newton, to school. He had it in his pocket the whole day, and when we got to strings class, Newton escaped and crawled into my cello case. I didn't even know about it until Miss Graham saw it. She screamed, then started yelling at me and . . . "

Bean continued her story. I nodded. I listened. My robotic processor tried to make meaning out of the events. Did she want my help? My agreement? My condolences? She seemed to forget about it as we entered a forest path that led through a park. Bean called it a shortcut, but despite being a more geographically direct route, it always took longer to cut through the woods.

"Someone found a bunch of guts sitting on a paper towel."

"That's terrible. Did they call the police?"

"It's just a story, Alek! Whenever kids walk through these woods, they tell stories. The guts were found outside those washrooms over there." Bean pointed to a small, grafittied building made of concrete. It had two metal doors with symbols for Men and Women. Not ever having needed those types of facilities, I had never been inside. I imagined it looked similar to the washroom at Bean's house.

"That toilet is cursed now; no one dares use it or something really bad will happen to you." Bean took a breath and continued, "and then there's the witch in the woodshed . . ."

"A witch in the woodshed?"

"Yes. That shed over there," Bean pointed to a decrepit wooden shed in a yard backing onto the park path. "There's a witch that lives there. She comes out after the bell rings to kidnap children who dawdle on the way to school."

"But that's just—"

"It's a story that makes kids get to school on time. I'm pretty sure a teacher or parent made that one up. And then there's the wolves."

"But wolves can roam up to twenty kilometres and this wooded lot is clearly not a large enough habitat."

"See those cages over there?" Bean ignored my comment and pointed to another backyard which had two enclosed, empty cages in the back corner.

"The dog cages?"

"No. Wolves. The man who lives there keeps wolves so that no one cuts through his yard. He lets them go if he catches you climbing the fence."

Bean's childhood seemed to be filled with peril and danger. I didn't understand what purpose the stories served, when she so clearly knew that they were just fairytales.

"You try one," Bean said, bouncing beside me on the pebbly path.

"Try what?"

"A story. Let me see . . ." She looked around as we walked. We passed a fire pit that obviously had been used recently. The smell of smoke still hung in the air. Ashes and blackened wood filled the pit. Cardboard cartons that used to hold beer bottles lay half-burned in the pile. One dirty running shoe lay on the ground beside the pit.

"There," Bean stopped, pointing to the fire pit. "Tell me a story about what happens here. At night," she added in a hushed whisper, her eyes widening.

I paused. I had never made up anything before. I was accustomed to facts, possibly hypotheses, but not completely made up tales. Could I do it? I decided to deduce a story.

"Last night a group of teenagers got together for a camp fire."

I glanced at Bean, who didn't look impressed. She was frowning a little. I added, "It was a dark and gloomy night."

The expression on Bean's face didn't change.

"The teenagers had stolen a case of alcoholic beverages from their parents' house. They had been drinking for quite a while and had become intoxicated." I looked around the scene and spied shards of glass lying on the ground next to some rocks. "They began doing foolish things, like throwing bottles against rocks. One of the shards flew up and hit someone in the ankle. He had to remove his shoe to inspect the wound more closely.

As he placed his foot on the ground, he stepped on a large piece of glass, which severely sliced his bare foot." I pointed out a brownish red stain smeared on one of the rocks. "This scene is a perfect example of the dangers of excessive drinking."

Bean stared at me.

"The end," I added. Bean frowned.

"We'll work on it," she told me, patting my arm. We resumed walking, now along the edge of the creek that meandered close to the path. Every now and then, Bean picked up a small stone or a stick and threw it in the current. At one point, she found a discarded Styrofoam tray. The object must have been there a while since the government had banned petroleum-based foam and replaced it with compostable, cornstarch-derived products. Bean picked up the small tray. Placing a sparkling pebble on top, she set the Styrofoam vessel carefully in the middle of the creek. She watched it for a while, walking along the banks while the tray weaved past waving weeds and sped up through the narrows between two large rocks. When the tray became lodged behind a dam of leaves, she gave it a nudge with her foot, and it continued on its journey. I was curious what purpose this activity served. Was it play? I decided to ask her.

"Why do you do that?"

"Do what?"

"Place a floating object in the water and follow it."

"I dunno." Bean stuck out her foot again and nudged the little boat, stuck behind a fallen branch. "It's fun. I like watching the water. I like predicting the path the boat will take. I like to see it speed up in the narrow water and slow down in the wide, deeper parts."

We continued walking, following the little boat until we reached a large drainage pipe sticking out of the side of one of the banks. Bean walked down the bank and hopped onto a large rock resting in front of the pipe opening. A small trickle of water dripped out to join the flowing creek.

"Hello?" she called out. Her voice echoed hollowly in the pipe. She stepped inside the pipe, ducking slightly. "Echo! Echo!" her voice overlapped and repeated.

"What are you doing?"

"It's cool in here! Come and see!" I gingerly stepped down the bank and onto the rock. I peered inside the pipe; Bean had walked about ten feet inside. The water and sun from the tunnel mouth played light across her face. She was smiling. I ducked down and stepped into the pipe.

"Say something." Bean instructed.

"Hello." I spoke. I heard my voice echoing back. It didn't sound like me. It sounded like someone speaking further down the pipe in the blackness.

"Look!" Bean pointed up where slats of light streamed in from a sewer grate. "I'll go up top. You stay down here and pretend to be an Invisible who lives in the sewers."

She scrambled past me, onto the rock, and up the bank before I could reason out the situation. I accessed Intelli!net for information on the subject: The Invisibles were a group of radicals living on the outskirts of society who rejected the way the government and large corporations had pushed for the majority of the population to be implanted with Intelli!chips. They claimed the implants were used not only for banking and information retrieval, but for tracking all citizens. Freed from their Intelli!plants, they removed themselves from society, sometimes living untracked in large cities or in their own isolated communities scattered across the abandoned suburbs.

The suburbs had become ghost towns due to large corporations preventing legislation that would ensure easy access to sustainable clean energy; the public transportation system couldn't keep up with suburban commuting demands when gas prices suddenly soared, tripling prices in less than a month. The media called it the Petroleum Parade; people fled the suburbs, abandoning their large, sprawling houses with expensive heating to live closer to their work in the city. The Invisibles had moved in, creating sustainable mini-communities where the commuters used to live.

Bean's head appeared over the grate. "Hello?" Bean spoke, "Is anyone down there?"

"Just me, an Invisible," I told her. I was catching on to imaginative play.

"No, you can't actually speak with words! Do some growling and weird noises."

"I'm not sure that I'm capable of that kind of vocal range."

"Just try it." Bean's head disappeared, then reappeared. She tossed a small pebble into the grate. It hit my arm with a clinking sound.

"What's that? Who's there?" Bean leaned down again, peering into the grate.

I tried to make strange sounds. "Oog gurgle smuck smuck groan growl."

"Ooh! It's an Invisible!"

"Sabine?" Another voice called from further away. Sabine's face disappeared.

"Oh. Hi, Russell!"

"What are you doing?" the other voice spoke, presumably Russell's.

"There's some weird man down here. I think he's an Invisible living in the sewer."

Two faces appeared in the grate.

"Hello?" Russell called out.

"Growl. Grawp. Smoot smoot smoot."

"Huh. Is that your dad?" Russell pressed his face closer to the grate. I backed into the shadows.

"Russsss-ellllllll" I spoke slowly, as I had seen the monster do on a horror movie Bean and I had watched one night when her parents were out.

"Who's there?" Russell's voice rose slightly, a sign of fear.

"Russss-ellllll. I am coming for your Intelli!chip. I will cut it out of your arm." I grabbed a stick lying on the bottom of the pipe and began dragging it along the corrugated sides. It made a scratching, echoey sound.

Russell's face disappeared and Bean said, "Russell, come back! It's only Alek!"

I lay down the stick and walked to the edge of the pipe. Bean and Russell appeared over the edge of the bank.

"What the hell, Bean!" Russell spoke shrilly. Bean started laughing.

"That was perfect, Alek!"

"I knew it was you," Russell huffed. "I just pretended to along with it."

He grabbed a rusted pail that lay next to the creek and dipped it into the water, then swiftly dumped it over Bean's head. Bean shrieked.

"Russell, I'll get you back for that!" She cupped her hands and tried to splash water at him. Alarmed at the building action, I attempted to step out of the way and onto a large rock jutting out. Suddenly my foot slipped on algae, and I toppled into the water, fully submerged. I quickly righted myself. I scanned my uploaded specs to see if I was waterproof and found I was water resistant, which evidently wasn't quite the same thing.

"Are you okay?" Bean, sopping wet, stood over me. "Here, help me get him out, Russ!"

Bean and Russell took my arms and guided me to the bank. Something was not right.

"I'm shorting out. My . . . legs . . ." My left leg dangled uselessly while my right stood stiffly, unwilling to bend.

"Oh geez, my mom and dad are gonna kill me!" Bean said.

"What are we going to do?"

Russell looked around. "How about this?" He pulled on a large piece of discarded cardboard. "We can pull him if he sits on it."

"Can you sit, Alek?" Bean asked me, pulling the cardboard up beside me.

I bent carefully at the waist and fell clumsily onto the homemade sleigh. The two children began pulling the cardboard, which slid slowly over the uneven ground. A few times I felt as if I were about to slip off the cardboard. My heels hung over the edge and dragged through the dirt. While travelling down a small incline, my entire body nearly slipped off sideways. When we reached the neighbourhood, Bean and Russell found it easier to pull me across the slippery grass on the boulevard rather than scrape the cardboard across the sidewalks.

"I feel like Dorothy from The Wizard of Oz," said Bean as she tugged. "I just wish I had an oilcan for the Tin Man here!"

"I . . . I am the . . . Tin Man?" I spoke laboriously; this was not a good sign.

"Of course. You're made of metal. You're obviously stuck because you're rusted."

"What does that make me?" Russell piped up. "The Scarecrow or the Cowardly Lion?"

"Oh, definitely the Scarecrow." Bean replied.

"Why? Because I have massive brains that I never knew I had?"

"No, because they don't meet the Lion until after they rescue Tin Man."

"Huh." Russell's voice betrayed his disappointment. What answer had he been hoping for?

"What happened?" Bean's father called as he came running out of the house. Evidently he had seen our procession from the window of his study.

"We were walking along the edge of the creek when Alek slipped and fell in the water." Bean spoke the half-truth breathlessly. She collapsed beside Russell, who had already fallen into an exhausted heap on the front lawn.

"How do you feel, Alek?" Sebastien crouched down beside me and stared into my eyes.

"My legs are shorting out. I . . . I . . . I. . ." The water had apparently seeped in to further wreak havoc with my processor.

"Dad!" Bean's voice was high and trembling. "He was talking the whole way here. It's getting worse!"

"Okay. We'll get him dried off." With a great effort, he picked me up and carried me into the house. Despite being the size of a grown adult, I wasn't as heavy.

Sebastien carried me into the front hall and set me down outside my recharging closet. Bean and Russell followed closely behind.

"Bean, get your mother's hairdryer in our bathroom. Russell, could you get some rags under the sink in the laundry room? It's down the hall to your right."

The two scampered away. Sebastien looked down at me.

"You don't have to do what she says, you know."

I stared at him, unable to answer, waiting for him to elaborate.

"Your job is to keep her safe, not to entertain her. Sometimes she forgets what you are. You are not a human playmate." Bean's father spoke kindly.

Russell came running around the corner with an armful of old towels.

"Start drying any parts that seem damp. Get into the creases if you can." Sebastien took one towel, and the two began drying parts of my body. Bean thumped down the stairs, hairdryer cord flying behind her.

"Here," her father said, handing her a towel and taking the hair dryer. "You wipe, I'll blow dry."

The hair dryer blasted noisily across my face, my chest, the joints of my appendages.

Ten minutes later, I could bend both knees.

Fifteen minutes later, I was able to stand up on my own.

Half an hour later, I spoke.

"I apologize, Dr. Sebastien. I did not foresee the possible hazards of the situation."

"Lesson learned. Stay away from water." Bean's father smiled at me.

"Thank you, oh Great and Powerful Wizard!" Bean bowed deeply to her father. He looked quizzically at the three of us.

"Don't ask me, I'm just the Scarecrow," Russell huffed.

"Oil . . ." I spoke as slowly and creakily as I could. I had done my research while being dried off.

4 / ANIMOSITY

The companions of our childhood always possess a certain power over our minds which hardly any later friend can obtain.

– Mary Shelley, *Frankenstein*

"SHE IS STILL so young," Sebastien's voice floated in from the living room.

"She's nearly twelve and quite brilliant! You've seen her teachers' comments."

"Yes, but socially, she's very immature. She doesn't interact much with children her own age. She spends much of her time alone."

"She's so far beyond the others that they can't relate to her. I had a similar experience as a young girl."

Bean's parents sat in the living room across from one another on matching chairs. Bean lay across the couch with her ear buds stuffed into her ears. I stood in the open charging closet, waiting at attention.

"Her birthday is coming up. Why don't we have a party and

invite a few children from her class?" Sebastien suggested.

"The balloons, the ultra-sweet cake, the silly games? No, I don't think so."

One rare thing that Bean and Catherine agreed upon was the subject of birthday parties. Bean felt uncomfortable being the centre of attention, and Catherine thought that self-planned home birthday parties were only for very young children and extremely tacky.

"Then see if she wants to invite a friend to one of our symphony outings. She really enjoys those," Sebastien said.

"She'll only invite that boy Russell. She needs to spend time with other young girls," Catherine insisted.

The conversation continued for several more minutes until Catherine nudged Bean, who removed her earbuds.

"Your father and I have come to a compromise on your birthday celebration. I will send out invitations to all the girls in your class. We'll call it a birthday soiree. It'll be more of a dinner party. Very grown up. It'll be lovely."

Bean groaned. "What about what I want? It is my birthday, after all. That doesn't sound like fun. Please, just take me out somewhere, just you and me and Dad."

"It's time you started spending time with other children your own age."

"I do, Russell and I go out sometimes and play—"

"No." Catherine interrupted. "I'm not talking about childhood playmates. You need a group of girls you can gossip with, talk about boys, do each other's hair."

"But I've never liked doing those kinds of things. I never will."

"You will learn. That's what pre-teenage girls do."

"Only if I can invite Russell too."

"You can't invite only one boy! How will Russell feel?"

"He won't mind. I want him there." Bean now stood in front of her parents, arms crossed in defiance. Catherine pressed her lips together in a thin line.

"Fine," she said finally.

"Fine," Bean echoed in the same tone. She stomped off. I heard her clomp up the stairs and slam her bedroom door shut.

"Those things that you say pre-teenage girls do, that's not exactly your experience as a young girl either, is it?" Sebastien spoke softly, putting a hand on Catherine's shoulder.

As usual, I was as overlooked as a side table, which was only acknowledged when one needed to find a place to rest one's glass. I stood impassively, monitoring the conversation, ready to spring into action at my next command.

Catherine shrugged off his hand, and moved to sit on the sofa. "No, and I paid for it. I had an awful childhood. I was teased for not doing the things all the other girls did. Instead of painting my nails, I was nailing parts together for a robotic arm. Instead of sharing secrets with a girlfriend, I was whispering voice commands into a wireless mic. I want Bean to be accepted."

"Have you explained that to her? How you felt as a girl?"

"Of course not! She'll just think I'm too old and far-removed from modern times. She doesn't understand how much my upbringing mirrors her own. I didn't want . . . I never wanted . . ." Her voice trailed off.

I quickly scanned Intelli!net, searching Catherine's family. Indeed, Catherine similarly grew up an only child, her brilliant parents were both highly respected in the scientific community and led groundbreaking research in the rock star world of quantum mechanics. While Catherine was attending university, they both died in an explosion set by a fanatic religious group who wanted to send a message about the dangers of interfering with what they believed to be "God's Blueprints of the Universe."

"Why don't you just talk to her? Share your experiences with her?" Sebastien said gently.

"She won't want to listen to me. I don't . . . I don't know how to talk to her." Catherine's face seemed to crack as her voice did the same. She stood quickly and walked from the room.

The invitations were sent out the next day.

Two weeks later, on the evening of Bean's birthday soiree, only four of the twelve students making up Bean's small grade six class had responded. Russell was the first to arrive.

Bean bounded to the door once I had opened it. She smiled widely at her friend.

"Hi, Russ," Bean said.

"Hi, Bean," he pulled uncomfortably at his shirt, which was buttoned up to his neck. "Happy Birthday." As he stepped into the doorway, three girls appeared behind him. They were giggling nervously and peering into the house.

"Welcome." I stepped forward. "Are you friends of Bean?" The girls looked at one another and burst into laughter. Bean hurried over.

"These are some girls from class: Rory, Steph, and Lisette." The girls looked past me, still peering into the house. They linked arms and marched past, short, medium, tall, brown, black, blonde, all different in appearance, yet identical in attitude.

"Happy Birthday, Beanie," the blonde short girl said as she passed. Bean flushed slightly. "So where's all the cool robotics and stuff, besides this thing here?" She gestured at me with a wave of her hand.

"You realize that Alek is a SimAid 3.3, Lisette? He's a Beta: his version hasn't even been officially released yet," jumped in Russell, who stood by Bean's side. "He's amazing."

"*Evidément*," said the one with black hair angled sharply around her face. She slowly looked me up and down. The other two giggled.

"Let's go downstairs," said Bean. "My dad set up the Simvironment system. We can go anywhere you want: the Eiffel Tower, the pyramids, Venice before it flooded."

"I've been everywhere in real life already," said Lisette, flipping her hair. "Steph takes me everywhere whenever her dad flies."

"Does your father pilot low-orbit commercial aircraft?" I asked politely. Steph startled, looking at me strangely.

"Why is it talking to me?" she whispered to Rory, the brown-haired girl.

"I think he's programmed to ask questions," Rory whispered back. I nodded.

"Have you been to Mars yet, Lisette?" Russell asked. She glared at him, then turned to Rory and Steph, rolling her eyes.

"*Quel imbécile*," she spoke, not quite in a whisper.

Catherine appeared in the doorway from the kitchen. "Welcome!" She spoke with a warmth and enthusiasm I had not heard before. "You must be Bean's school friends."

The girls turned to Catherine, all smiling widely. "Are you Bean's mother? But you're so much younger-looking than my mother!" said Lisette. Catherine giggled much in the same manner as the girls and smoothed the front of her skirt.

"Very nice to meet you, Dr. Archambault. Where is the other Dr. Archambault?" Rory asked politely.

"He's downstairs synching the visors for the Simvironment. You're in for a treat."

"Oooh – I can't wait!" squealed Steph.

I couldn't understand the change in their attitudes. Moments ago, they had been uninterested in the game. The girls followed Russell and Bean downstairs. Catherine turned to me.

"Um, Alek. . ." She still had a hard time using my name. "You will need to set the table for seven with the formal silverware in the dining room hutch."

"Yes, ma'am."

I dutifully set the table and made the necessary preparations for the meal. In honour of Bean's special day, I had made her favourite homemade pasta and vegetarian sauce, garlic bread, and Caesar salad. Catherine, not trusting me to demonstrate the proper artistic flair when it came to festive desserts, had ordered the cake from a local bakery. I had timed the food preparation so that it was all ready simultaneously.

"Go fetch the other children and inform them that dinner is ready. Please," she added awkwardly.

"Yes, Ma'am." I walked into the basement. Bean and Russell were plugged into the Simvironment system, oblivious to my presence. Lisette, Steph, and Rory were nowhere to be found. I tapped the two gamers gently, to avoid alarming them.

"Dr. Archambault would like you to make your way up to the dining room for dinner."

"Good, 'cause I'm starving!" Russell removed his helmet and helped Bean with hers. Bean smiled at me as she went by.

"Thanks, Alek."

Looking around the room for the others, I became aware of voices coming from the bathroom.

I walked over to the closed door and found it locked.

"This is so *tragique*," said a voice sounding like Lisette. "My parents made me come, just 'cause they work with her parents. They're like genius freaks or something at TARIA."

"Yeah," chimed in another, probably Steph, "but she talks like a baby and plays babyish games all the time. I heard that she plays dress up and wears costumes around the house!"

"She's so *tellement* weird. She carts around that huge instrument all day long. It's, like, so uncool."

"Her parents are never home," Rory's voice cut in. "She just plays with that robot. I kind of feel sorry for her."

"What kind of kid plays with robots all day? She's got no friends. She thinks she's too good for us.

"Her hair is a disaster. I don't think she even brushes it, like, ever."

"I like her hair. It's beautiful in a natural sort of way."

Someone snorted.

"Maybe we should give her a little help." The door opened, and I stepped to the side.

"What are you doing there, SimAid?" It was Steph.

"We are serving dinner in the dining room." I said formally, in the only way I knew how. Rory shot me a quick, guilty look as the others filed by.

The guests filed into the dining room and sat around the large table. Goblets of sparkling grape juice and bright white napkins hemmed in gold were placed at each setting. Had I been able to feel surprise, I would have felt it at the sight of Catherine carrying in a large salad bowl on her own.

"I'll serve the salad. Alek, go and grab the bread from the oven."

Forty-five minutes and several helpings later, Bean's guests sat fidgeting in their seats. Much to Catherine's disappointment, the dinner conversation evolved from which teachers were the meanest to which boys were the funniest class clowns, and finally to a dare involving pasta being sucked in by mouth and out through nostrils.

I noticed Bean laughing as she watched Russell play with a particularly long string of spaghetti, pulling it back and forth like a piece of dental floss.

Sebastien interrupted the contest with the announcement of cake. As I brought out the platter, the children erupted into what I presumed to be a rather multi-keyed, raucous rendition of "Happy Birthday."

As was the birthday custom, Bean had requested donations to a local charity. This year, she had chosen Musical Wishes, a charity that provided instruments and music lessons to underprivileged children. After Bean went online to a special site set up for her birthday donations, and thanking her guests and their parents for their contributions, the girls suggested visiting Bean's room.

"I've gotta go, Bean. I have fencing practice in half an hour.

Thanks for inviting me."

"Thanks for coming, Russ."

As Russell walked to the front door, I retrieved his coat from the closet and handed it to him.

"Thanks, Alek. See you around. Bye Dr. and Dr. Archambault. Thanks for everything," he called into the other room. Sebastien joined us in the hallway and shook Russell's hand.

"You're welcome, Russ. You're a good friend to Bean." Russell blushed.

"Well, goodbye." I closed the door behind him and went back into the kitchen to clean up.

Despite the large amount of food consumed, there was still a lot left over. I packaged up the remains of the pasta and sauce and put them in the fridge. As I began clearing the table, I noticed a small red purse that had been left hanging over the back of one of the chairs. I removed it and walked upstairs to Bean's room to return the item to one of the girls. Just before knocking, I paused upon hearing Bean's voice.

"I don't think that's a good idea."

"Don't think, Sabine," Lisette cut in sharply. "Just let us do the work."

"Look," I could hear Rory saying, her voice trembling slightly. "I think maybe we should just go. It was fun at first, but this is too much."

"Yeah, Lisette," Steph added, speaking tentatively. "This is getting sorta boring."

The girls jumped from the bed as the door swung open and I stood, holding the purse in my hand.

A few locks of Bean's curly auburn hair lay on the floor. Her eyes were ringed in vicious black lines, and her lids were layered in bright green. A slash of red covered her lips and continued halfway up her cheek. Rory held up a phone close to her face, presumably taking a picture.

"Go back to the kitchen, SimAid," Lisette growled, gripping a pair of scissors, which glinted sharply in the light. Just then, Sebastien came into Sabine's room.

"Hey, there's still some cake left if—" he stopped when he saw his daughter. He stared, taking in her garish makeup, the phone, and the group of girls frozen like mannequins around Bean.

"Give me the phone," Sebastien held out his hand.

"It's my own personal property," Steph whined. "You can't take it from me." Sebastien took a breath and looked to his daughter. Bean shook her head almost imperceptibly.

"If I hear that any pictures were posted of this night, I will contact each of your parents. I think it's time for you all to leave. Now."

He spoke quietly, but his words hit them like a slap. They scampered off the bed and squeezed between us and through the door.

"Bye, Sabine. See you on Monday." Lisette spit the words from her mouth like a threat, then grabbed the purse from me as she passed. The group stomped noisily down the stairs, opened the front door and slammed it shut behind them. Sebastien sat down on the bed, shoving a pile of cosmetics aside.

"Bean, I'm sorry . . ."

"Go away." She spoke softly, staring straight ahead, not looking at either of us.

"I just want to see if—"

"Go away." Bean spoke more loudly. Her brow furrowed and tears appeared heavy and ready to spill from her eyes. Sebastien sighed and got up from the bed. He turned to her before leaving the room.

"I'm here if you want to talk."

I followed him out as he closed the door behind him. We heard a shifting on the bed, then muffled sobs. Sebastien's face crumpled in apparent pain. He turned and walked into his room, shutting the door. I continued to stand behind the closed door, listening impassively, on the verge of comprehension. Despite that I could not yet feel them myself, I could identify emotions based on physical signs; but their cause was often beyond my understanding.

Days in the household stood out sharply but identically, like toy soldiers at attention. With an electronic brain, I continually had a date and time stamp on any event that took place. I could tell you exactly how many times the phone rang and who had called. I knew when the laundry cycle finished and the dryer began. I was able to list at what time each duty was completed throughout the day. I calculated the distance and speed needed to pick up Bean from school on time and walk her home. I was activated, I performed my duties, I retired to my charging closet, again and again, day after day. But I wasn't bored - how could I be? Does a coffee maker tire of its endless steaming and percolating at precisely the same time every morning? To be bored would require an awareness of wanting things to be different, to be more.

5 / AWAKENING

Here it is—a piece of common firewood, good only to burn in the stove, the same as any other. Yet—might someone be hidden in it?

– Carlo Collodi, *The Adventures of Pinocchio*

WHAT IS A year in human awareness? Someone once explained to me how time changes as you grow older. For children, it is the long space between birthday cakes, another notch on the growth chart in the doorway. A year for children stretches out into infinite possibility. A summer between school years is an eternity; a special weekend at the zoo is made sweeter by the eager anticipation leading up to it.

As an adult, the time condenses and a year becomes a span of time to reflect upon what has been accomplished and what has been neglected. There is a continual shortage of time: twenty-four hours is not enough to complete a day's work. After five days of work, the weekend is barely time to refresh.

I prefer a child's perception of time.

A year of school days and holidays came and went. I shovelled my first snow, decorated my first Christmas tree, planted my first spring bulbs—but all these firsts were lost on me. My routine varied slightly depending on the season, but it was still just that: a routine and a duty.

Bean had become increasingly isolated from her peers after the unflattering photos taken at her birthday soiree circulated within her small school community. She began to spend more time at home, a SimAid her only companion.

It was a chilly afternoon at the end of the school day. The trees were bare and the sky was beginning to go grey with the early winter twilight's approach. I stood, mechanically pushing Bean on the tire swing in the backyard. I couldn't understand it then, the enjoyment that someone could possibly acquire from moving back and forth within the same space, not really going anywhere. Bean, however, loved this pastime. Sometimes her eyes remained open and alert; other times, she swung with her eyes closed, a quiet smile on her face.

"Bean," I began.

"Yes?" Her eyes were still closed, but her head tilted slightly towards the sound of my voice, her ear angled to me.

"Why are you an only child?"

She opened her eyes. "What do you mean?"

"You don't have any siblings. I've observed that most families contain two or more children. Do your parents plan to have more?"

Bean stuck out her feet so that the swing came to a rapid stop. Her eyebrows inched together slowly, thinking.

"Well, I don't know if my parents had planned to have any

children at all, but here I am."

"What do you mean? Didn't your parents understand what is required to conceive a child?"

Bean's cheeks turned slightly pink. She looked down at the toes of her dusty shoes. "Uh. I'm pretty sure they know. You'd have to ask them about that one. I mean, no! Don't. . . don't ask!" she added.

So asking personal questions about conception was not an acceptable topic of small talk - another conversational nuance that I needed to learn.

"Besides, you're with me." She looked up at my face and smiled slightly.

"But I am not a suitable companion."

"Yes, you are! I like that you really listen to what I have to say. I like that you ask me questions that most people wouldn't think of asking. Besides, you're a good swing pusher, and you're always willing to play whatever I want."

I thought about this for about a nanosecond. "You like that I'm different."

"Yes. Sometimes . . ." she paused. I waited. ". . . Sometimes I feel like I'm different too. I don't always understand the kids at school—why they do certain things and say certain things. You make me feel . . . normal."

If I'd been human, this thought would have been disturbing, but at the time, I accepted it. I began to push Bean again, her black shoes and black jeans swinging like a pendulum.

"What's it like, being a robot?" Bean asked me after a minute.

"It is like nothing. I am a robot," I answered. How do the blind describe lack of sight to someone who can see? How could

I explain more? It was all that I knew, then. There wasn't yet a consciousness behind the thought.

"What is it like being human?" I asked her; my social programming again caused me to mirror questions back to the other person.

Bean pressed her feet into the ground and stopped the swing. She looked up at the darkening sky for a moment. "It's like," she paused and thought again. "It's like swinging. You know you're attached to something, but sometimes it feels like you could just fly away. Or it's like dancing. If you start to think about it instead of just doing it, you mess up the rhythm. You can't think too hard about it. You just have to do it."

I nodded, still understanding nothing.

I awoke abruptly, unsure of my surroundings. I wasn't in the charging closet. Strange. I knew I wasn't scheduled for a maintenance checkup for another week. I was lying on a metal table. I attempted to sit up, but discovered that I was unable to move. I found I was able to swivel my visual receptors slightly. I looked around to find myself in a small room, nearly quiet except for a faint humming in the background, nearly empty except for an array of machinery, tools and a computer terminal to my left.

Suddenly, I detected the shadow of a presence hovering just above my head. I looked up and saw the back of someone's head, a mass of black curls, a long and oversized plaid shirt over a pair of baggy jeans. Behind his shoulder, on an otherwise bare wall, a poster read:

The limits of the possible can only be defined by
going beyond them into the impossible.
- Arthur C. Clarke

"Implantation complete."

It was the voice from my initial memory before coming to the household. The head turned, and I saw a man's bespectacled face change from a look of concentration to surprise as he noticed me awake.

"Oops!" he sucked in his breath and came rushing towards me, touched a panel on the back of my neck and—

I was in the Archambault house again, plugged into my charging closet in the front hallway. It was dark and quiet, except for the slow and constant ticking of an antique grandfather clock. I could tell it was slowing down by milliseconds and would need winding in another week. I looked around cautiously. A fluffy feline leg poked through the crack in the open door, pawing curiously at my feet. I shifted my foot and the paw disappeared. Two green eyes glowed in the dark, reflecting the tiny glow from my recharge indicator. Timpani. The cat often wound himself around my legs, and I'm sure would have jumped up on me if ever I had the need to sit. The green eyes quickly disappeared then reappeared in a blink. With a last swish of his puffed tail, he evaporated into the darkness.

I scanned my time stamp for a present date and time, then scanned my history for time I had spent in the unfamiliar room. Nothing. I knew that it was presently 6:30 a.m., my usual activation time, but I didn't have any record of being moved. The strange memory stood out starkly, a fragment that remained after everything else around it had been erased. How unusual.

I unplugged myself and took a step. Stranger still, I had a sudden feeling of . . . discordance. I momentarily was unsure of where to place my feet. It was the oddest sensation, something that I had never experienced. It was as if I had forgotten the steps for walking, unsure of the moment to shift my balance from one side of my body to the other.

I began noticing the smallest things first.

Every morning, as was my routine, I made breakfast and then accessed the Intelli!net news broadcast on the kitchen wall by the breakfast bar. The phone rang. I swiped away the news and answered the call. The screen indicated that the incoming call was from the customer feedback department of TARIA.

"Happy New Year. Archambault residence."

"Is this a SimAid or a real person?" Something in my head twinged at the question. A momentary glitch, I assumed.

"I am Alek, a SimAid," I answered. "May I ask who is calling?

"Goodness it's hard to tell the difference nowadays. What happened to robots sounding like robots?" the voice on the other end complained. My voice sounded human, yet still lacked a complete range of expression, something that programmers were still working on. I am always astounded at what an array of emotions the human larynx can convey. I had difficulty vocalizing anything other than the required pleasant subservience. "Why is your visaphone not up?" the voice continued.

"I have been instructed not to turn on the visaphone until

after 8:30 a.m."

Catherine didn't like to be seen in the morning before she had assembled herself, as she called it. It seemed hard work for a human to fully wake up. Much time was spent in the bathroom. I simply activated and was ready to go for the day.

"May I ask who is calling?" I repeated patiently. What else could I be but patient? Impatience was reserved for those who lived for a future moment that never came. Robots are always working on a task at hand.

"It's Susan Dominico from TARIA. I was calling to get some feedback on how the Archalmbault's new 3.3 is functioning."

"I'm fine," I told her. There was silence for a moment or two.

"You're . . . fine?"

"Yes. Is that not the appropriate response to an individual's inquiry of your overall health and wellbeing?"

"Well, I suppose so, but I really wanted to talk to one of the Doctors Archambault about how they feel it . . . ah, you . . . are fitting into the Intelli!home, if you're performing your duties sufficiently."

"I can assure you that I am."

"But—"

"You are aware that, as a SimAid, I am no more capable of lying than I am of feeling the need to exaggerate or boast about my usefulness?"

"Yes, uh. All right. Please ask them to call me back or send me a message." The call ended and the Intelli!screen read: Call Ended by TARIA/Customer Feedback.

My processor felt hot. As I turned to the refrigerator to record the required inventory of the day, I heard a quiet, staticky sound, like the white noise of radio transmissions from the universe. I glanced over at the Intelli!screen, but it was turned off. As I walked through the kitchen, the sound followed me. I turned around, but nothing seemed out of the ordinary. The noise continued for most of the morning: a small, background hum accompanying my daily chores.

Bean and I lay on top of the plush living room carpet playing chess. We were 47 minutes into the game, ten minutes past the average time that Bean lost focus and became impulsive with her moves. If I distracted her too much, I would win. I had learned to play a careful game: let her lose enough times that when she won, it felt like a hard-earned victory.

"I want to know where you came up with my name."

"Alek?"

"Yes, of course," I said impatiently. I paused. Impatience? When had I ever felt that a human couldn't think or speak quickly enough? It had never bothered me before. I was aware that the human brain worked more slowly. My brain, on the other hand, was constantly running multiple background processes and answering almost instantaneously. I had noticed lately that if I had to wait for an answer, I had nothing left to do but focus on that moment.

Bean sat thinking. I wasn't sure whether she was planning her next few moves or pondering the question I had just asked.

"It's a name I called all my teddy bears and stuffed animals at one time or another, any goldfish that lasted more than a week, and the odd stray dog that came wandering into the yard. They were all Alek, I guess. It would have been either Alek or Brownie Brownpaws, depending on the day."

"I'm glad you picked Alek that day."

"Me too," Bean breathed out in a huff.

So I was a stuffed toy, a stray dog, a house pet. I didn't mind. How could I? Yet somewhere inside me, something prickled.

"Check," announced Bean. "You're not letting me win again, are you?"

"I'm playing at a standard 13.2-year-old level," I replied.

"So you're letting me win," she said, disappointment creeping into her voice.

"Technically not," I argued. "If I'm running a program at a specific experience level, I could beat you. But this time, I didn't. You outplayed me."

"You're going to have to start playing up a level," Bean huffed with her head down, but I could see a satisfied smile behind her curtain of hair.

My mind reached back to pull a memory of the previous chess game with Bean. I had won and she had seemed excessively upset about it. I remembered how she had flipped the board and all the pieces had gone flying. Several had bounced hard but harmlessly off my face, and Bean looked momentarily worried until she remembered that I couldn't feel pain. She left the room quickly after that. Bean later told me of what a horrible school day she'd had, of how someone had snatched her Intelli!pad when she wasn't looking and hid it in the lost and found. A teacher had yelled at Bean for coming in late to class after looking for her lost Intelli!pad, then Bean's Intelli!chip couldn't access her school account so she wasn't able to pay for lunch. I understood how Bean must have been feeling by the end of that day and realized that I should have let her win the chess game.

Lately my mind had often become occupied with reliving some event, imagining how it might have turned out differently, or considered a future occurrence and how it might eventually play out. I had a hard time focusing on the present moment, and it made me feel dissatisfied.

6 / ANXIETY

THE YOUNGER THE child, the easier it is to see time's stamp on their bodies. Babies transform into little people; their small, fat limbs grow lean and stretch out at an amazing speed, as their bodies continually shed proteins and cells, their hair and nails grow longer and periodically need to be trimmed.

Humans are fixated on the passing of time. You can witness the phenomenon of time's effects sped up on countless Intelli!Me videos. Video diaries of physical aging show hairstyles changing five times a second, lines appearing on the face like rivers on a map, decades of gravity's pull weighing down skin: years transform human beings before your eyes.

More months passed. As Bean began to stretch out, so did the time she spent alone. Her parents increasingly put more time into their lab work, their meetings at TARIA. Some days

I didn't see them at all.

Unlike regular school days when Bean and I returned home to an empty house, one Thursday we returned home to her parents entertaining a visitor. As I closed the front door, Bean's father walked over to us and the visitor stood up quickly, his curly, bouncing hair mirroring the energy he seemed to exude. I recognized him immediately as the individual I had seen that night I awoke outside of my charging closet. I made the sudden and inexplicable decision to say nothing. Not a lie, of course. I was incapable of lying.

Wasn't I?

"Bean, I'd like you to meet Dr. Trent." Bean's father motioned for Bean to step forward. "He works with me in Robotics Research at TARIA."

"Hello," Bean said politely. She was accustomed to her parents unusual colleagues, who seemed to talk of nothing but quantum mechanics, neuroengineering, and nanotechnology. As Trent shook her hand briefly, he looked over her head at me. Bean continued staring at Trent, a small frown on her face, then gasped and said, "Oh! You're the one who won the award last year! You're Alek's dad!"

"Who?"

"This is Alek," Bean told him, before her mother could call me by my factory number. Catherine only called me by my name in front of her daughter, and always with the expression of someone biting into a lemon.

Trent stared at me as if I was the first robot he'd ever seen. Odd, considering he worked with the greatest and latest in technology, not to mention that fact that he had seen me that night. I was sure of it.

"Alek, it is a pleasure to meet you. You must be a third generation model. The first out from the factory, I'm thinking."

"Among the first," Bean's father answered, as I stood mutely, trying to determine if I had a place in this conversation. "But I'm sure you know him inside and out. It's your baby."

"That it is," Trent nodded in agreement. He peered into my face. "Tell me, Alek. Do you prefer Alek to your factory number?"

He was looking for something. He wanted a particular answer from me. I could tell by the way he didn't take his eyes off me.

"I am pleased by the name of Alek if it pleases the Archambault family."

The corners of Trent's mouth dropped and his eyes narrowed.

"He does what he's told," Catherine spoke curtly. "He's a SimAid. What do you expect?"

"Yes, yes. We were, however, experimenting with a new SimEmote program. The SimAid 3.3's should be able to detect and emulate appropriate emotional reactions."

"Oh?" Sebastien's eyebrows raised in surprise. "More than simply mirroring facial expressions?"

"Well, yes," Trent looked uncomfortable for a moment. "Uh, but just with a few of the models. I knew you were getting this one. You'd be able to keep me up to date on its progress."

I looked to Bean. She frowned slightly. A minute ago, Trent had been guessing at my model, but now he was saying he knew exactly which SimAid the Archambaults were getting?

Sebastien looked confused. "He's been with us for over

two years. When exactly were you going to tell us about these updates?"

"Well, I didn't want his progress to be impeded by any unnatural reactions towards him. We want first to establish firmly his SimEmote program."

Bean's parents glanced briefly at one another in an expression I couldn't read.

"But he's not . . . it's not actually feeling, is it?" Catherine said, as if switching pronouns could negate what was happening to me.

"Oh, no. Of course not, what I meant was that . . . that is, I mean to say, Alek is learning responses that imitate human emotion. It's a lengthy, complicated process for a SimAid processor. He's registering changes in voice and facial expressions. That . . . kind of . . . thing," his voice drifted off.

Trent's stuttering gave away a lie. Was I the only one to notice? His eyes darted around the group, not quite looking at anyone, but over our shoulders at the sparsely decorated walls. I suddenly felt something I hadn't experienced before. If I had been equipped with a biological body, I would have experienced a fizzy bubbling in my chest. My eyes would have opened wider. My heart, I imagined, would have started pounding faster.

I think it was fear.

The fourth year of my existence continued similarly to the first three, but with an obvious difference. Time seemed to expand and contract depending on the moment. I no longer experienced it as the reliable, measured beat counting out the universe's steady progress towards entropy.

I kept track of the days by their differences. Anything outside of my routine stood out clearly in my memory. Regular daily rituals seemed to bleed one into another. My internal date and time stamp began to malfunction. I was no longer certain of the exact date of past events. Inexplicably, I had developed a sense of dread at the thought of being sent to the lab. Most SimAid updates were delivered wirelessly by Intelli!net, which I was no longer getting, since my Intelli!net connection became sporadic, unpredictable. I told no one.

When the connection was strong, I began scouring the entire network for information that fascinated me. Despite their desperate need for power and control deriving from a fear-driven survival instinct, the human race had accomplished spectacular and beautiful things. Language and all of its nuances and uses was of particular interest to me. I read everything, the entire works of Shakespeare, T.S. Elliot's poetry, Douglas Adams' Hitchhiker trilogy in five parts, and Dr. Seuss. I also uploaded great works of art, watched dance performances, and viewed theatre pieces from across human history, trying to understand their purpose.

As I greedily absorbed the data, it began to change me in small, unquantifiable ways. I could not explain it, but I felt different. Yet despite my abundance of knowledge, I felt as though I was missing some crucial understanding that was just beyond my grasp.

As my connection to Intelli!net inexplicably worsened, my uploading of humanity's failings and accomplishments slowed.

Still, I learned much of its vile history of subjugation, of one group asserting its fictional superiority over another group, of the shame and humiliation inflicted upon those whose skin shone a different blush, who lived technologically innocent lives, who were the wide-eyed young. Hopelessness and despair was smeared upon their souls as thick as the blood and dirt on their bodies.

Trent started to visit once a month. He would ask his odd questions of me, then leave with obvious disappointment. Catherine always hovered nearby.

Bean continued to play the cello in her room, sometimes for hours. She mainly kept to herself, but occasionally played with Russell. Her thirteenth birthday came and went. To celebrate, her parents took her to the symphony, as she had wanted.

One night after Trent's monthly visit, I carefully loaded the dishwasher and Bean stood at the sink, washing the pots and pans. Despite the amazing technological advances of our modern society, certain dishes still needed to be washed by hand. I kept far away from any dealings with water after my Tin Man experience.

The kitchen was dark except for a light above the sink. The house was quiet since Bean's parents had gone out with Trent for dinner to discuss TARIA politics. Despite that loading the dishwasher while Bean washed dishes was a common after-dinner scene, somehow tonight it felt different. I sensed from Bean something that could only be described as calm. We did not talk. We did not communicate at all, except when a plate passed between our hands. Yet, I felt a comfort, a near pleasure, in the routine, in the quiet. How could that be? And then, almost as if I had voiced these ideas aloud, Bean spoke.

"You're different."

"What do you mean?" I turned slowly in the direction of the sink.

"I mean, I think Adam Trent's SimEmote program is working. You seem more, well, emotional."

"Can you give me an example?"

"The other day I noticed while you were talking on the phone that something the other person said irritated you. You paused before speaking, like you actually had to think of how to say something appropriate. Also, when I play my cello for you lately, I swear you are enjoying it!"

"You're becoming a very good cellist."

"Yes, but any other SimAid wouldn't be getting pleasure out of music. What's going on?"

I didn't have to think very long to decide that Bean was the one person I could talk to.

"Something's happening. I feel it," I told her as I closed the dishwasher door. "You're right. I do feel impatient at times, and irritated, and happy. At least, that's what I think it is. It's not as if I've ever experienced anything with which to compare it. But it's not a program."

"What do you mean?" Bean frowned, draping a dishcloth over the sink tap.

"It is not a programmed outward response to a situation. I am having some kind of inward . . . reaction. I don't always know why or how I'm feeling. Sometimes my thoughts wander. I find myself thinking about something that has happened or imagining how some future event will unfold. The other day while I was cooking dinner, I started thinking back to our last chess match and wondered if I could have beaten you had I not sacrificed my bishop so early. I lost track of time and almost burned the chicken roasting in the oven. I forget about the present moment. It makes me feel . . . dissatisfied."

"What could it be?"

"I don't know. There is something that Dr. Trent isn't telling your parents. I had seen him before he started coming to the house. I was in his lab, and he didn't mention it."

"Well, sure, if he was your inventor, you might have early memories of him from the factory."

"No!" I stopped, startled at the vehemence I was able to express in that one word. Bean's expression mirrored my own astonishment.

"No," I continued more quietly. "It's more recently than that. I've awoken in the middle of the night and I'm not in my charging closet—I'm in his lab. He's been there." I felt urgently that Bean needed to understand that Trent wasn't being entirely truthful. "I don't want to tell him how I really feel. What if it's a mistake of his programming? Something he didn't expect? I . . . I like the changes."

"Are you afraid he'll try to change you back? Do you think he'd shut you down?" Bean whispered the last question as she looked worriedly into my face. I experienced a primal, instinctive response even without the benefit of physiological reaction.

"I don't want to die."

7 / AMBIDEXTERITY

TRENT WAS BACK. I could hear him in the living room arguing with Catherine. Bean put a finger to her lips then motioned me closer to hear. I stood beside my charging closet in the hallway, listening in.

". . . Just think, Catherine, we'll be at the forefront of the movement! Advances in bioengineering have slowed. It's become the stuff of puttering basement laboratories. We need to do something revolutionary."

"Yes, but the Committee for Ethical Science—"

"If we wait for the green light from the Ethics Committee, we'll be throwing out years of work! The time is now."

"But why are you suddenly in such a hurry?" A pause.

"What, and let some other scientific community in another part of the world beat us to the punch?"

Catherine sighed. "As long as it's just a pair of hands."

Hands? Were they talking about me? I looked down at my clunky, metal polymer sensors. Bean looked up at me with curiosity plainly etched on her face.

"We've already done the preliminary testing. There should be no problem keeping the tissues alive and connecting the nerve endings to his electronic sensors. Just think of the possibilities!"

I heard Catherine take another deep breath in and out. I peered quietly around the corner. Trent's face was alight with some strange, feverish excitement. He looked practically ill.

"All right. Just the hands."

"It's a start," he told her, smiling broadly. They spun around as Bean's head bumped into the hallway Intelli!screen, and it beeped questioningly, giving our position away. Bean walked rapidly into the living room to give the impression that we had just arrived.

"Hi Mom, I'm home! I—oh!" She looked at Trent with surprise that I could tell was faked by her exaggerated expression.

"You remember Adam Trent, Sabine? He's here to . . ." she trailed off."

"To discuss some wonderful new improvements to your . . . uh . . . to Alek!" Trent quickly finished.

"Is this a common upgrade?" Bean asked innocently.

"No. Only a select few. Well, actually," Trent cleared his throat, "only Alek. Your mother and I will be working closely to monitor his progress. He will be installed with human hands."

"Whose?"

"Pardon?"

"Whose hands?" Bean folded her arms.

"Oh, no! It's not as though I'm removing a person's hands and sewing them on. I'm not Dr. Frankenstein, you know!" Trent laughed, more loudly than seemed appropriate. Catherine joined in heartily. The humour of Trent's comment escaped me.

"Alek's hands will be created in a bioreactor that facilitates tissue and bone regeneration. We've been working on a pair of them for the past year. They should be ready next month."

"We'll be the only family to have a SimAid with real functioning hands. Isn't that exciting?" Bean's mother pulled the corners of her mouth into a smile.

"Wow! What do you think, Alek?" Bean turned to me. Catherine and Trent stared at me.

"Whatever pleases the Archambault family pleases me." Trent's expression told me I had not answered as he had hoped.

"But how do you feel about it, Alek?" Trent prodded.

Again, something big was hinging on my answer. I felt an immediate need to leave the room.

"If human hands will help to increase my usefulness to the family, then it is a positive upgrade." I kept my voice neutral. Trent frowned as Bean took my arm.

"Come on, Alek. I need a snack." I followed her out to the kitchen.

Bean sat at the kitchen counter eating peanut butter and bananas on crackers. I had cut the bananas and set out the crackers, but Bean had spread the peanut butter herself. A small pile of crumbs and broken cracker bits, casualties of my imperfect engineering, were strewn like shrapnel across the counter; I had difficulties trying to gauge the precise pressure required to spread the peanut butter with a knife without breaking the cracker.

"You know," Bean spoke through her stuck mouth, "you wouldn't break crackers with new hands."

"True," I agreed as I began clearing away the battlefield with a damp cloth.

"And you'd be able to pet Timpani properly," Bean grabbed her copper-coloured cat, who had long ago given up his protest against Bean's sudden attacks.

"What do you feel?" she asked, thrusting the creature towards me. I slowly reached out a hand. Timpani let out a quiet warning moan. He had never liked me much; to him, I was a walking microwave oven, a moving stairway, a piece of furniture that ought to stay in one place but didn't. As I lay my hands on his back, he bucked in Beans arms, but Bean held him tight. My fingertip and palm sensors indicated an object that emitted an elevated temperature compared to the air in the room, and whose surface gave way slightly under my hand,

"I don't know what I should feel. I know it's a cat. It's alive."

"He's so soft and warm," Bean purred at Timpani as she held him to her face and rubbed his fur with her cheek and scratched him behind the ears. Both girl and cat's eyes were closed. As I observed cat and girl mutually enjoying the touch of one another, I became aware of an odd sensation: a longing for what I could not yet experience.

I was scheduled for hand transplantation two months later.

Sebastien dropped me off at Adam Trent's TARIA workspace, which I immediately recognized as the lab from my unexpected nighttime awakening. The only difference in the quiet room was that another poster had been added to the wall. The new one read:

> *Technology is a word that describes something*
> *that doesn't work yet.*
> - Douglas Adams

I understood the irony of the quotation and was mildly surprised to discover that Trent had a sense of humour.

Sebastien sat down in a chair facing Trent's large and unkempt desk. His eyes swept around the room, looking at the equipment and posters, looking everywhere but at me. I stood to the side of the door since it would have been unusual for anyone to ask me to sit down.

Moments later, Trent appeared at the door. Sebastien rose from his chair and the two men shook hands.

"Thank you for bringing him in, Sebastien. I should have him back by tomorrow, providing the preliminary tests are successful."

"That's just fine. Good luck, Alek," Sebastien nodded in my direction.

"I would shake your hand," I said to him, "But I don't have any yet."

Both men stopped and stared at me. Trent burst into laughter, and Sebastien smiled weakly, backing out into the hallway. "All right then. See you tomorrow."

"That was funny, Alek!" Trent proclaimed, and I felt as though I had just passed some secret exam I didn't even know I had taken.

Trent asked me to lie down on the metal table, and I obeyed. He talked to me while fiddling with my metal hands, turning to the counter every so often to grab a different tool.

"I'm beginning to think that your upgrades are becoming fully integrated. I wasn't sure the last time I saw you that everything was going smoothly, but your last comment gives me hope, Alek. Have you noticed any changes in your reaction to people and situations?"

"Could you please clarify, Dr. Trent?"

"Do you, uh, feel judgment associated with any events? A negative or positive sensation?"

How long could I keep these changes to myself? I decided to tell him a version of the truth: a change that he seemed to anticipate. "I feel different things lately. From what I've learned, I can only describe them as emotional reactions."

Trent stopped working on my hands and stared intently into my face. "Such as?"

I felt a growing fear that I imagined surging though my non-biological body. I'd have to tread carefully, not reveal too much. "Pleasure upon being complimented on a meal that I've prepared. Annoyance at breaks in Intelli!net connectivity. It doesn't happen all the time."

Trent studied my face carefully, as if trying to see past my metallic mask into my processor.

"Ah. Any negative reactions to . . . people?"

"No. I enjoy serving the Archambault family. Whatever

pleases—"

"Yes, yes," spoke Trent quickly. I could see the frustration plainly on his face. "Whatever pleases them pleases you." He turned away from me to grab a small screwdriver from the counter and resumed his work on my hands.

"What about any sounds that you can't explain? Do you ever hear a buzzing sound that has no obvious environmental source?"

I was surprised at that question. "Yes, actually. Occasionally I hear a buzzing sound that almost seems as though it is coming from inside of my head."

Trent stopped and leaned forward, looking keenly at me. "When did it start?"

"I would say about six months ago."

"Precisely six months?"

"I . . ." Strangely, I couldn't pinpoint the exact time when I first heard it. Normally I could check a time stamp, but there didn't seem to be any. "I'm not certain."

"Hmm." Trent slowly smiled. "Tinnitus."

"Isn't that a human inner ear condition caused by neurons firing in the brain?"

"Yes." Trent's eyes widened. "But it could be a similar robotic, uh, glitch, where you are simply reacting to, uh, electrical activity in your pro-processor." He was stuttering again: a sure sign of his lies.

What was going on?

"I will have to deactivate you while I replace your hands. That way I'll be able to do some testing of your reaction with the bio-hands before you attempt to control them yourself."

I said nothing. It was not as if he needed my approval; my body was not my own.

Trent opened up my chest and inputted a series of codes on the small control panel. "See you on the other side," he said. Just before I faded out, I caught a glimpse of Catherine walking into the room. She wore her lab coat and a grim smile.

Nothingness.

When I was awakened in the lab seven hours later, my processor felt burdened and sluggish. It was not until I felt a tingling sensation in my lower arms that I remembered my hands: my glorious, human hands.

Living flesh! Kept fresh and alive with a tiny mechanical pump and purifier just under my wrists that circulated the synthetic blood. Biological nerve endings were attached to the sensors at the end of my arm; I felt tiny electrical jolts of sensation, much more exquisite than a scientist could ever create from scratch.

I held my palms up close to my ocular receptors. I wiggled each finger in turn. I closed my hands into a fist. I turned them over, running my fingertips over the knuckles of my opposite hand. I even had nails to trim. I took a sheet and draped it over my robotic arms so that only my hands were visible: soft-looking, slightly pink from the capillaries underneath, folds where the joints bend. Human hands. I turn my hands over looking at the long, strong fingers, not as strong as my metal appendages, but a new kind of strength in their sensitivity. I brought them close to my face and followed the whorls on the fingertips. My very own fingerprints like no one else's. I traced the shadowy lines in the palm of my right hand with my left: little roadways in the skin. I felt as though my insides were glowing.

I was transfixed.

A few days later, as I dusted the shelves in the library, my hand paused as I identified the title on the spine of one of the books: Mary Shelley's *Frankenstein*. I opened the pages and quickly scanned the first few chapters. The reference that Adam Trent had made when Bean had asked him about using somebody's human hands: that reference made me the monster.

I shut the book quickly, and in doing so, I sliced my index finger with the edge of a page: a paper cut. I had been told that I didn't feel pain in the way full-humans did, but the nerve endings sent a message of mild alarm to my processor. It wasn't pleasant. I looked down at the tiny slit; a small amount of synthetic blood, red and realistic, bubbled up at the edge. I placed the book back on the shelf and hurried up to Bean's room, bursting in without knocking, holding the cut hand out from my body. She looked up and stopped writing in her journal.

"I'm injured. My hand."

"What?" Bean jumped up, dropping her pen and notebook. "Let me see!" She grabbed my whole hand and turned it over. "Where?"

"Here." I curled up my remaining fingers and held out the injured one, as if pointing at her. Bean gingerly touched it and bent down for a closer look. She straightened up and burst into laughter.

"What's so funny?"

"It's so tiny! What happened?"

"I got a paper cut."

"Ooh! Those are the worst! I think you'll be fine though."

"But . . . do I heal? Will it get infected and spread?" Bean's smile transformed into a look of concern.

"I don't know. Let's ask Dad."

After activating an Intelli!home search on the !screen in Bean's room, we learned that her father was in his study. I followed Bean across the hall. She knocked on the study door.

"Come in," came a muffled voice. Bean opened the door to the small room. Sebastien was at his desk with his head in his hands. He looked tired. As Bean explained what had happened, her father lifted his head and swivelled his chair to face me.

"Let me see . . . It looks clean. I think it should be fine. We can put a little antibiotic on it just in case. It's a fully functioning hand, though, as Trent said, so it should heal on its own."

Fascinated, I stared at my finger for the next hour, as if I could see the healing in progress.

How could I have imagined what joy real hands would bring me? This emotion puzzled me. How was I experiencing it? This sensation did not seem like an emotional simulation program. It didn't feel like my regularly running processes. I placed my palms together, as if in prayer. I could sense the slight warmth emanating from one hand to the other. I folded my fingers down, clasping. These are my hands, I thought to myself. These are my *hands*.

These are *my* hands.

How often in a day do human beings use their hands to

greet each other, express appreciation for one another, show affection? How often do they hurt and curse and push away with those same hands? I made a vow to myself never to use my hands in that manner. I held one injured hand in the other as though cradling a sacred gift.

Scientists had long ago found ways around the human body's rejection of donated organs and body parts, which it considered to be a foreign intrusion. However, adding biological parts to a machine was a different matter. Trent was concerned about whether the hands would accept the mechanical. My hands were examined weekly to ensure successful integration. I was growing accustomed to their heightened sensitivity. I couldn't have explained it, even to Bean, but somehow I felt a deeper connection to my hands than to the rest of my body.

I decided to attempt handwriting. Bean couldn't help much because it was no longer taught in schools, considered more an art than a practical skill since everyone learned keyboarding and !net navigation skills from the time they could sit up. I found a pen in the junk drawer of the kitchen and ripped a piece of paper from an old notebook. Pulling up a sample of a handwritten alphabet on the Intelli!screen, I copied the letters several times. Next, I slowly started scribing my name. Alek. Alek. Over and over. My first attempts looked nothing like the sample, but after several minutes, my letters began to take shape. Bean walked in from school with her cello case strung over her back.

"What are you doing?"

"I thought I'd try my hand at handwriting."

Somehow, I felt rather foolish admitting this, but Bean set her cello case on the floor and plunked down on a stool beside me.

"Cool. Can I try?" She found another pen in the junk drawer and began scrawling her name, first and last. Sabine Archambault. Bean Archambault. Her name flowed from her pen over and over. We both leaned down over our paper and wrote and wrote.

After a few minutes, Bean looked over at my page.

"Yours is neater."

"Mine is easier. You've got a first and a last name. I only have one."

"You could be an Archambault since you're part of this family."

I couldn't look at her face. She really didn't understand.

"There's a difference between being part of a family and belonging to a family."

"Of course you belong!"

"No," I sensed frustration in my attempts to explain, and something more. "I don't belong. I am owned. I'm the property of your family."

Bean sat quietly for a moment.

"I don't see you that way," she whispered. She scrubbed at her face, then picked up her pen and began writing furiously.

Minutes later, she stopped again. "Are you a righty or a lefty?"

"Pardon me?"

"Do you write more easily with your left or your right hand?"

I thought for a moment. I just happened to reach for the pen with my right hand, since that was where the drawer was located.

"Let's see . . ." I switched hands and began writing with my left. At first, my writing looked similar to the right hand's first attempts, but gradually, my left hand caught up with my right.

"You're ambidextrous, I guess," said Bean. "That's rare."

"Like my hands."

Bean looked at me, staring for a moment at my head, then down to my hands.

"More than rare," she spoke slowly. "I think your hands are pretty much unique."

We looked back down to our filled pages. Bean's page was filled with a multitude of sentences, fragments, exclamation marks and dashes, and half-completed thoughts. I found beauty in her words. I caught sight of the words belonging and hands. It was a definition:

Belonging: to be owned by, be the property of,
be held by, be in the hands of.

I liked the sound of the last one: to be in the hands of.

I had written my own name over and over, perfectly spaced, on every line. It reminded me of the ancient punishments I'd seen depicted on reruns of old television shows, where a student wrote endlessly, righting a wrong they'd committed at school.

8 / AWARENESS

IN THE SUMMER, Saturday was market day. Catherine liked me to accompany Bean to the farmers' market to buy produce while she spent more time in the lab. Today was the first market day with my human hands; now I would be capable of picking out the freshest fruits and vegetables. I could squeeze gently to detect the exact firmness of a tomato's flesh, the perfect give of a just-ripe peach. I began wearing gloves, not only to dampen the sometimes overwhelming sensations from my hands, but to prevent gawking. People reacted to my human appendages as though they were a pair of disembodied hands from a horror movie.

Even though I could now choose produce myself, Bean accompanied me out of habit. Since the banning of harmful chemical pesticides to treat crops, produce became more varied in quality. Bean enjoyed the challenge of haggling with the stall vendors, trying to talk down the price of a broccoli bunch, playfully arguing until an agreed price was reached. I'm not sure who had more fun, the vendors or Bean.

At fourteen, Bean was tall, not quite sure enough of herself to demonstrate grace, but when she forgot to think about her body, her mind shone. She had convinced her parents after much argument and negotiation to let her leave the Cummings School for the Gifted for a fresh start. She had never recovered socially from the photos that went viral after the birthday incident involving the trio of girls.

Her parents agreed to enrol her in the local public high school. Its large population ensured that Bean could remain relatively anonymous, yet at the same time find a group of like-minded students with similar passions. Russell, the "ever-present mutual misfit," as Bean often referred to him, had joined her at the public school. The two remained friends, and hung around a ragtag collection of budding musicians, spending all their spare time in the large, airy music room, or crammed into one of the attached rehearsal studios.

Bean talked more often about her new high school friends than she ever had about the students at the Cummings School: Kate, a flute player whose bubbly and outgoing personality immediately drew Bean to her; Shawn, a funny violinist whose whispered wisecracks had Bean stifling giggles in the middle of rehearsal; and Kimber, a dedicated percussionist who never stopped moving to the music constantly playing in her earbuds and who loved to talk intensely with Bean on any subject.

As abruptly as her entry into the public high school, Bean's outward appearance changed. She was not a caterpillar making the slow and painful transformation into a butterfly; she was more like a human body skinned and turned inside out. She was still Bean, but violently unrecognizable. Bean began armouring herself with sarcastic humour, joking complaints, to mask the things that really bothered her, the things she was afraid of. She was afraid of people not taking notice of her, or of them taking notice of her for the wrong reasons, so she dressed to detract attention. Her dilemma was this: how to get noticed without giving away any of the real Sabine. The clothing she wore wouldn't cause her to blend into a crowd; but she didn't dress provocatively, only to cover up. Striped stockings covered legs ending in heavy boots like army tanks; layers of dark clothing concealed her body; her blackened nails often beetle-scurried through hair that was unnatural shades of green, red or blue—sometimes an entire rainbow. She pierced her face in several places as would a fearsome ancient warrior, but strangely, wore no makeup at all. She must have been afraid to draw too much attention to it. It was hard to hide the hurt and abandonment behind her eyes. Her lips could break out into unexpected offerings of such wide, sudden smiles, but tugged at the corners when she thought no one was looking. All her natural softness was filed into toughened edges by steel toes, ragged hems and bluntly cut hair. Look at this, she seemed to be saying, but don't look at me.

She rubbed her nose with her index finger if she felt someone was examining her too closely. Her hair was her Sampson strength—while it was kept long, it was her confidence and her shield. She laughed when complaining, to dampen negativity.

But she was just Bean to me.

The vendors were accustomed to this odd-looking teenager and her virtual companion. Today we were adding to our motley crew by meeting up with two of Bean's friends, who were just coming from an early morning drumming session at a local coffee shop. After hugging them enthusiastically, Bean introduced me to Kimber and Shawn.

"Hey, Alek," Kimber nodded, adjusting the djembe slung over her back. I nodded back.

"Alek, what's new?" said Shawn, looking up at me curiously through the blonde shaggy hair swaying in front of his eyes.

"These!" Bean grabbed my hands and displayed them proudly.

"Whoa," Shawn said, slouching to squint at my hands. He resembled a camel with the pair of bongos hanging between his shoulders. He straightened up.

"That's amazing. High five!" He held up his hand towards me at the level of his head. I slapped it rather awkwardly with my right hand. Everyone laughed.

"We'll work on it," Shawn reassured me, nodding sagely.

We walked over to Bean's favourite local farmer's stall. A young woman wearing jeans and a peasant top stood under a tarp, a rainbow collection of fruits and vegetables were displayed across the wooden table.

"Good morning, Bean!" the woman greeted her with a wide smile, her small nose stud catching the light. They shook hands; Bean's own hands were short-nailed and calloused from playing the cello, and the farmer's were similarly short-nailed and calloused from working in the earth.

"Amanda, these are my friends, Shawn and Kimber."

"Hello. You must be freakishly talented and wonderfully kind as well," she spoke to the pair.

Shawn grinned and bowed. Kimber smiled shyly.

"What lovely produce," Kimber said, running her hands over a basket filled with dark, plump plums.

"Thank you," the woman leaned in closer and whispered, "the secret is in the loving contact you give the plants and thinking thriving vibes. They need to be petted, just like a cat or a dog."

"Really?" Shawn raised his eyebrows. "Do you name them all too?"

"Hey, Amanda," Bean interrupted. "Alek has something to show you."

She nudged me, and I pulled off my gloves and handed them to Bean, who shoved them in her pocket. Amanda gasped. She did not, however, look horrified or disgusted. She seemed to be intrigued.

"Oh, Alek! How lovely!" She grabbed my hands and turned them over, feeling the fingers and pressing into my palms. "How do they feel?"

"Well, there are a bundle of nerve fibres attached to my own sensors which emit—" Amanda laughed heartily, cutting me off.

"No, I mean what do you think of them?"

"The sensations are much more detailed than with my old hands."

"They look very realistic." She said, lightly pinching the skin on my knuckles.

"That's because they are," Bean told her. Amanda, Shawn, and Kimber all looked surprised.

"What do you mean?" Kimber asked.

"My hands are made from human biological material grown

in a laboratory. They are not," I paused, "used. They're new."

"Well, that's terrific. I'm very happy for your new upgrade." Amanda smiled at me. Bean lifted a peach out of a basket.

"Feel this." She handed it to me.

I gingerly held the peach in my open palm. I wasn't sure what to do with it.

"Put your fingers around it," she instructed. "Press the skin." I rolled the fruit around in my hand and gently pressed it with the tips of my fingers; it felt cool, soft, fuzzy. The flesh gave way a little under pressure.

"Oops!" My thumb had pierced the peach and was firmly stuck in the fruit. Juice dripped down my wrist.

"That's okay," Amanda said. "It just takes practice."

"Remind me not to let you hold my newborn cousin," Shawn added.

Bean took the peach from my hand and took a bite. "Mmm. We'll take this basket." I watched her chewing the fruit in obvious enjoyment, wondering what it would be like to taste something.

After choosing the basket of peaches, a bag of mushrooms, and a bundle of carrots, Amanda calculated the total.

"That'll be 11.25." Bean pulled her sleeve up to scan the Intelli!plant in her wrist.

"It's kind of ironic, isn't it?" I said.

"What is?" Bean asked, tugging her sleeve down over her wrist.

"That you have a piece of technology in you that I don't have." I held out my hands and turned them over, wrists up. "Your hands are more robot than mine now. I mean, I can't pay for things with my wrists."

Shawn smirked. "That would be a good excuse if you were on a date and didn't want to buy dinner."

Bean's face turned inexplicably pink as Kimber and Amanda giggled.

"Let's not forget I don't actually eat." I replied.

Kimber and Amanda laughed louder, but Bean turned her face away.

"Bye, Amanda. Have a great day," she said, a strange note in her voice, falsely bright, but with another tone underneath that I couldn't quite identify.

"This has been fun," Kimber said, but I've got to get home and finish my English essay for Porter's class."

"Yeah, I guess I've got to start mine," Shawn said reluctantly. Kimber looked at him in disbelief.

"You haven't started yet?"

"I figured I'd whip it up this afternoon." Kimber rolled her eyes.

"See you, Bean. Nice to meet you, Alek!"

"Bye, Bean. Alek, if you ever need a good manicure, I know this girl who's fabulous," Shawn exclaimed mockingly. Bean grinned.

"Bye! See you at practice Monday morning." As Shawn and Kimber walked towards the bus stop, Bean and I sauntered around the market.

This morning we noticed a new stall set up at the end of the parking lot. Its wooden struts were covered in brightly coloured fabric. A hand-painted sign read:

Alana Bell. Present explained. Future revealed.

"Let's get your fortune read!" said Bean, a mischievous spark in her eyes.

"But I'm not . . . I don't—" I began.

"What? You don't have a future to tell? She's a scam artist anyway," Bean scoffed. "It'll be worth it just to see the look on her face when you sit down."

"But she won't give me a reading," I insisted. "She'll take one look at me and throw us out."

"Even though she'll know right away you're different, I bet she'll give you a reading anyway just to make her money. Come on." She pulled me into a gap between the silks.

The tent was small and dark. Although I could see instantly despite the sudden lack of daylight, I waited beside Bean for several moments until her own eyes adjusted to the dimness. A woman sat at a table with two empty chairs across from her. Her chin was down as she sat gazing at an unseen spot on the table. Incense overpowered the air, but other than that, the room contained none of the usual trappings of a fortune-teller's space. No candles, no crystal ball. The woman wore a plain, hooded sweatshirt with a pair of jeans. Her straight black hair was wound up in a scarf in the same material of the tent's multicoloured walls. Her head turned almost mechanically in our direction. She smiled widely.

"Welcome! You are my first customers! I'll give you a free reading as long as you promise to tell your friends and family about me."

"Sure," said Bean, smirking. "But not me. Just him."

"Sit," the woman instructed, and we sat in the empty chairs.

The fortune-teller closed her eyes briefly, then opened them and fixed at a space just above my eyes. I realized what was different about her.

"You're blind."

Beside me, Bean let out a small gasp.

"I don't need eyes to see into you," she spoke gruffly.

"But why don't you get implants?" I asked her. "Why choose to be blind?"

"When I lost my eyesight, I gained my inner sight. Pretty fair trade-off if you ask me. Sometimes when we look at other people with our eyes, we don't see what's really there."

Bean nodded, then remembering the woman couldn't see her, said, "Yes. That makes sense."

The fortune-teller cocked her head to one side, as her unseeing eyes stared beyond me. She looked a bit like a quizzical bird.

"You're not a coffee drinker, are you." It was more of a statement. "You have the aura of someone without an addiction wearing you down."

I waited patiently, mildly curious. What could this woman tell me about myself? She held out her hands. After a moment's hesitation, I placed my hands on top of her own. Her fingers and thumbs curled around and pressed down where the pulse of my wrists would be if I'd had a proper circulatory system. She gasped, withdrawing her hands from mine as if they had been dipped in acid; she opened her eyes widely, the eyeballs rolling crazily in their sockets.

"But you . . . you're. . ."

"He was built originally as a SimAid, but he's going biological," Bean told her simply. The woman tentatively took her hands again and placed them on top of my own.

"You have. . . you are connected," she began. "Words can't really describe the feeling; but you are, well, in computer terms, you're plugged into the Source.

"The Source?" Bean said, her eyebrows raised doubtfully.

"The Source of all Life, the Collective Unconscious, the Universe, God. Call it what you will. There is an interconnectedness to all of humanity. Whether we are conscious of our link to each other or not, it's there; it exists. And you," her sightless eyes widened in amazement, "You are linked, integrated into the system. I can feel it in you."

I sat stunned. Some part of me was human. She felt it. I had felt it. I wasn't just a mass of circuits encased in an artificial body. I was becoming . . . more!

We all sat silently for several moments, marveling at this revelation. Then Bean spoke up.

"What about the future?"

"Bah!" the woman looked disgustedly in the direction of Bean's voice. "Garbage! That's just a bunch of nonsense to get the tourists in. I have a gift, you know, but no one wants to hear about themselves now. It's all about what's going to happen. If they only knew how undefined, how imperfect and flexible the future is, they would focus more on what they can do right now with their lives instead of always focusing on some hopeful distant thing. The Now is where it's at." She focused her attention on me. "You have been given a gift. You are unique, yet you are like billions of us now. Don't squander it."

Bean looked at me, something indefinable shining in her eyes. The entire trip home, I kept catching her sidelong glances, a quick turn of her head as she peered out from behind her hair, and finally her blatant stares. Several times she opened her mouth to speak, only to close it again.

"I knew it," she breathed finally while we rode the bus.

"What?"

"That there's something going on with you. You're not just some mindless automaton!"

"But what's going on? I feel . . . different, than I used to feel. I feel, oh," I paused frustrated. "I don't know how to explain it! I feel more than I used to."

"It's because you're more than just a belonging, Alek. You do belong."

"Explain that to your parents," I said in a low tone.

My hands were the talk of the town. Adam Trent and the Archambaults were interviewed in various scientific journals, but I managed to stay out of the line of fire. No one would think to ask a computer how it felt about its new upgrades. However, I continued wearing gloves to prevent people from stopping to ask if they were real, did they once belong to someone else, and how could they get the same upgrade for their SimAid. The Archambaults hosted a variety of dinners in their home, inviting fellow TARIA and visiting experts in fields of Robotics and Human Regeneration. My hands were both the servers of their meal and the object of their discussion. I was touched, examined, talked about, talked over, but never directly talked to. Not that I expected anyone to ask me; yet I couldn't help but feel bothered by it. Then Adam Trent appeared at the house one evening, and he alone looked me in the eye and spoke directly to me.

"How are the hands working out, Alek?" Catherine stared at him as if he had sprouted antennae.

"Adam, I don't think—" Trent cut her off with a wave of his

hand.

"Well?" he said. "Do you notice any differences in your functioning? In your abilities? How do you feel?"

I spoke carefully. "I am able to detect more minute differences in the texture and malleability of objects. I've sensed no discomfort and have experienced no problems with integration." I thought for a millisecond before adding, "And I've honed my fine motor skills, such as handwriting."

Catherine frowned in confusion. Sebastien's eyebrows raised. "You've practiced handwriting?"

"Yes," Bean cut in. "He's ambidextrous."

"How fascinating," Trent's eyes widened and sparkled. "What use would it be to your everyday functioning?"

I knew then that I had made a mistake. "I . . . I thought that the practice would help overall with fine muscle control."

"Hmm." Trent walked around me in a slow, tight circle. He looked over my shoulder at Catherine, who stood like a stone statue, one hand on the back of an armchair.

"And what would you say to eyes?" Trent whispered close to the side of my head, where my ears would be. I turned to look at him.

"Eyes?"

"We could do wonderful things," Trent spoke, a gleam in his eyes. He stifled a cough.

Catherine stepped forward, "You didn't mention anything about such a complex organ, which would be directly linked to . . . to what?"

"Trust me," Trent said.

I felt my hands tighten, unbidden, into fists.

9 / ACUITY

Might it be that this piece of wood has learned to weep and cry like a child? I can hardly believe it.
– Carl Collodi, *The Adventures of Pinocchio*

MY EYES WERE placed into my skull like smooth river stones. Shining and slick, they were taken from a dead woman and a dead man, husband and wife, who died when the car they were driving was hit head on by a transport truck. The driver had fallen asleep at the wheel. Ironically, he was fine except for a head injury that rendered him blind, despite his eyes remaining intact. The couple's bodies were destroyed, all but a left and a right eye: one blue with brown specks—a Caribbean shoreline tumbling bits of shell and pebbles; one yellowy-green—a cat's eye marble. I became disconcerting to people who met me for the first time, having two different-coloured eyes staring at them from a metallic face. Their own eyes shifted focus from one to the other, uncertain of where to look. They settled on the middle of my humanoid face, my suggestion of a nose, or sometimes my forehead; but I could see their eyes flitting back to mine, a car crash that they couldn't quite look away from. I ended up having to wear a strip of plastic around my eyes to prevent others from seeing in, shielding them from my strange appearance. I was reminded of the similarly-visored Geordi from old episodes of Star Trek: The Next Generation, except that his visor not only shielded others from his unseeing, cloudy eyes, but also gave him sight.

I became a strange chimera, a mixture of biology and science that people weren't quite able to accept.

It may sound gruesome to you that I had taken the sight from the dead, but they found new life through me. I could see now with imperfect eyes, made perfect by the sheer fact that they were human. I no longer saw the infrared and ultraviolet in the spectrum; the colourful constraints of a rainbow made detectable colour much more significant now.

Sight was not as precise, everything looked a little softer around the edges, filled with more life and not as starkly contrasted. I gave up the acuity of a hawk and gained an artist's perception.

"Field trip," Bean announced one morning through a mouthful of crumbling toast. It was a P.D. day for Bean's school.

"Where are we going?" I asked her curiously. She waggled her eyebrows comically.

"You'll see."

At the Light Rapid Transit station, we met up with a band friend of Bean's, who immediately looked me in the eyes, despite measuring a full foot shorter than me, and introduced herself enthusiastically.

"Kate. I'm a flautist." She pursed her lips as if to demonstrate, and tilted her head to one side, smiling up at me. Her thick brown hair brushed the tops of her shoulders. "You must be Alek. It's great to meet you! Are you going to be helping us with our Visual Art History assignment?"

I glanced over at Bean, who smiled encouragingly.

"Bean hasn't told me where we're going," I told her. "I'm happy to help if I can."

An LRT ride later, we stood at the front doors of the Art Gallery of Ontario, its large, vaulted entrance like a subway station opening up into the bright and airy Walker Court.

"Three students, please," Bean spoke to the attendant once we had approached the counter. The attendant glanced at me then gave Bean a strange look.

"There's no charge for, uh, help," she said significantly, looking back at me with a confused look.

"Oh . . . of course." Bean rifled through her bag in a flustered kind of way, then pulled the sleeve up above her wrist to scan her Intelli!plant. The attendant handed Bean the printed ticket.

"Thank you." Bean hurriedly took the ticket and pulled me past the ticket counter. "Enjoy your visit to the AGO," the attendant called to us. I turned swiftly, lowering my visor, and gave her a small wink. She gasped and turned to nudge the attendant working beside her, but he was working with a visitor. An elderly man sitting at the roped-off entrance scanned Bean's and Kate's tickets without a second glance at me, and we walked on.

"Can you believe that some people don't get an Intelli!plant, or even carve out their implants once they're in their arms?" Kate shivered in apparent revulsion.

"I can see their point," said Bean. "They feel as though they're constantly being tracked. They think their privacy and sense of individuality is being compromised."

"What, are you turning Invisible?" Kate teased. Bean stuck out her tongue.

The Invisibles were worried that not only could major corporations and the government find out what individuals were up to on social media, but when the Intelli!chips replaced banking cards, then driver's licences, health cards, and all other identification people used, anyone who had access to Intelli!chip info could determine the present and exact location of an individual. It wasn't exactly illegal not to have an Intelli!plant, but it was difficult to do everyday things without one. Most businesses didn't accept credit or debit cards anymore and only scanned Intelli!plants.

In the first room, we were introduced to Kathleen Munn, Canadian pioneer of abstraction, who looked the part of the typical Canadian artist of the 1920s. In her photograph, she wore a loose-fitting man's shirt and dress pants in quiet rebellion against the socially imposed dress-code of her gender. Her hair was escaping the bun, tendrils caught in a frozen dance about her face. She was looking at something off in the distance, a paintbrush gripped between her teeth, a large palate cradled like a child in her arms. I walked around the room, eyes on her paintings lining the walls. From far away, I clearly saw *Cows on a Hillside*. Up close, it became brushed squares of colour. The paint looked newly applied, the strokes standing out on the canvas. Kate giggled as I walked closer and backed up farther away several times, at one point, bumping into a young couple.

"Sorry." I ignored their stares and concentrated again on the painting.

"I imagine you're doing exactly what Munn did, walking back and forth between painting and standing back to look at her work," Bean observed.

In another darkened room, the artwork on the walls were spotlit like actors on stage who had suddenly frozen, forgetting a cue. The scenes and people in the paintings looked so lifelike; the paintings seemed like a doorway into another world. Faces were highlighted with some unknown light source. Their expressions of passion, anguish, betrayal, joy, and serenity were clearly etched on their faces. I surreptitiously removed a glove and brought my hand of flesh to my metal face. Oh, that I could express as clearly outwardly what I was feeling inwardly!

The Henry Moore sculpture centre was filled with large masses of bronze and concrete. I felt as though I was walking through an ancient battlefield strewn with the bleached bones of giants. I stood before *Warrior with Shield*. He was cast roughly in bronze, not shiny or smooth. He was missing his left arm, left leg, and a right foot. His chest was broad, his shield held out in front of it. On his small, and nearly featureless head, his eyes were two holes that stood out like the eyelets of a boot. He seemed familiar, somehow, but slightly off, like looking at a reverse reflection in a mirror.

I laughed aloud with delight.

"I get it!" I crowed.

"Get what?" Bean asked.

"Art," I explained. "I've never been able to see it this way before. It's always been blobs of paint, brush lines, faces, light and dark, but never like this. It makes me . . . joyful. Let's see some more."

We spent the afternoon racing from one painting to the next. I wanted to laugh, cry, astounded at these strangers and their ability to make me feel something. We ran our hands across sculptures when the guards' backs were turned, we made fun of modern art installations such as *A Large Piece of Furniture Partially Obstructing Doorway* or an untitled work that depicted a wad of chewing gum stretching from floor to ceiling.

"I don't understand all art," I admitted.

"No one does." Bean patted me on the hand.

"I'm adding my own art installation," Kate announced, kicking off a shoe. It skidded to a stop by a guard standing in the corner, who glared at her.

"I call it *Forlorn Shoe Lying in Silence*," she laughed and grabbed her shoe, sliding it back on her foot. Kate pulled on Bean's arm, hurrying away before the guard came after them.

We climbed the curling DNA strand of a staircase, huffing and puffing by the time we got to the very top floor. Evan Penny's strangely stretched out sculpture of an incredibly realistic looking face, complete with skin pores and stubble and shining eyes greeted us, towering over ten feet high. It stared at me as if to challenge what I was seeing. I dare you to make sense of this, it said.

I found myself now able to appreciate the artists' ability to force the eye to look a certain way, in a certain direction. I was able to take in images and colours gradually with the sequencing of a story rather than everything all at once. I'd seen paintings by the Group of Seven in books. They always seemed a jumble of colour and shapes, nothing standing out to my electric eyes, which took in everything. They were not programmed to seek meaning, only detect colour, movement, distance, and identify objects. Now I really saw. A story unfolded as my eyes swept over the canvas: a windswept tree, rocks by a wintery lake, a sunset sky seeping into darkness. I understood the mood being created with each brushstroke.

"They make you slow down and look . . . I mean really look at things, don't you think?" Bean said, admiring Emily Carr's red cedars stretching up into the sky.

On our way home, I stared out the window, my eyes taking in the swiftly moving landscape as our train moved silently across it. Art, art, art, whispered the part of my brain that took in the uniform row houses that marched neatly past, the tottery pile of ancient cars in a junkyard, the plowed fields quilting the hills in newly sprouted greens, and behind it all, the quiet reflection of a crazy-haired girl in the window. I found that I could study Bean without her realizing it. Instead of looking beyond the window, I focussed on her reflected green eyes, the curve of her lips, the bit of blue hair tucked behind an ear.

Art, came the whispered voice again. Beauty was everywhere if one stopped to take notice of it.

Bean and Kimber sat in the kitchen one day, Bean's feet no longer swinging on the high stool, since her legs had grown long and now touched the floor. Wearing an intent look on her angular face, Kimber shared her earbuds with Bean to let her listen to a particularly challenging piece of music they'd been struggling to compose and perform for a class project.

"Here." Kimber beat with a complex rhythm on her knees. "That's where you come in to emphasize the downbeat." As they listened, they munched on the after-school snack I had prepared for them: a bowl of hummus and pita triangles. Bean's parents were still at work.

"I get it," Bean said. "It's a little jarring, but it works."

"Now if we can just get Russell and Shawn to be serious for one minute and get their parts down," Kimber said, her black eyebrows arching. Bean grinned.

"But you know they always pull through at the last moment."

"True," Kimber nodded seriously, readjusting her earbuds. "Let's listen again."

As I prepared dinner, Bean and Kimber put away their earbuds and began their math homework.

"What's the after-tax total if I buy three items for $8.99 each and one item for $4.99?" Bean asked me innocently over her Intelli!pad.

"Are you allowed to ask help from Alek?" Kimber asked, frowning.

"You are supposed to figure that out. It's your homework, not mine," I told Bean as I placed a pan to heat on the stove.

"But I'm doing the work at home. You're part of our household. Isn't it fair that you help me?"

"If by helping you mean giving you the answer to the question, then no." I couldn't help doing the computation quickly in my head, however. Despite my continued problems with my wandering focus and Intelli!net connectivity, I still retained my computational skills.

"How about geography, then?"

"No."

"Biology?"

I smiled and reached for the cutting board. "I think you know more than me by experience alone in that category."

She sniffed, hiding a smile.

"All right. How about English Literature? That's always good for discussion. And with no right answers, I'm sure you'll find it interesting."

"What do you mean, no right answers?" I called from inside the pantry, then reappeared with two onions. "Are you staying for dinner, Kimber?"

Kimber glanced at the Intelli!screen clock, "Actually, I've got to get going. My parents are going out tonight and I have to babysit my little sister." She grabbed her backpack and stood up. "See you tomorrow, Bean."

"I'll let you out." The two girls walked to the front door, had a short conversation and said goodbye. As Bean returned to the kitchen, I repeated my question.

"What did you mean about English Literature having no right answers?"

"That's the great thing about English Lit," she said, sitting down again at the breakfast bar. "You can talk for hours about themes and characters' motivations and not really come up with any definite answers. Take *Romeo and Juliet* and one of its main themes, for example."

> *"Two households, both alike in dignity*
> *In fair Verona, where we lay our scene*
> *From ancient grudge break to new mutiny*

Where civil blood makes civil hands unclean.
From forth the fatal loins of these two foes
A pair of star-cross'd lovers take their life . . . " I intoned.

"Have you got the whole play memorized?" Bean asked me, frowning.

"Intelli!net," I answered, tapping my head, yet I could still sense that my connection was more sporadic than ever before.

To hide my uncertainty, I asked, "What do you consider the main theme?"

"Destiny," said Bean in her melodramatic voice, low and grand.

"What about it?" I asked, pulling a knife out of the drawer.

"Well, do you believe that everything that happens to us is predetermined? That we have no control over the outcome? How does one live like that? By simply accepting everything that happens to you as something that was meant to be?"

I thought about the concept of destiny. Was I predestined to become human? Bean kept talking. "Don't you wonder what your destiny is? I mean, here you are, on the frontier of making human history, and you're stuck with me and my messed up self."

"You're not messed up. You're . . . you're my Dorothy."

She snorted. A lovely sound.

"What do you mean?"

"I'm the Tin Man. You're my friend. With me all the way. I don't know what I'd do if you weren't . . . "

"Weren't what?" she said softly.

"Weren't supporting me on this . . . journey. Does that bother you? Are you embarrassed by me?" I felt my hands grow hot.

"No! You understand me more than anyone else. I just wish

others saw you the way I do."

"How do you see me?" I spoke quietly.

"I see you for what you could be."

"What exactly could I be?" I asked her placidly, hiding my growing frustration.

"Sometimes you are infuriatingly calm and logical. It's that side of you that's not really you."

I looked down and began to chop the onions more vigorously than needed. She gasped, "That's what it is! You get all strange and mute when you think people are examining you, judging you. My gosh, Alek, I am just having a conversation. There is no right answer."

"Then why do I feel whatever answer I give you is wrong?"

Bean sighed in exasperation. "It's not that. You try too hard to find the right answer.

Suddenly, my eyesight became blurry and a sharp, stinging sensation caused my eyes to squeeze shut.

"Ugh!" I shouted and dropped the knife.

"What is it?" Bean hopped up and came over to my side.

"My eyes! They burn!"

Bean was quiet. I couldn't see what she was doing. I heard her begin to laugh.

"Why are you laughing? This hurts!"

"It's the onion juice. It makes your eyes sting and water."

"When will it go away?"

"Give it a moment." I could hear Bean sliding the cutting board covered with the offending vegetable away from me. "I'll finish it up for you."

"How do people cut onions without this horrible reaction?"

"My grandma used to wear swimming goggles. I've also heard chewing peppermint gum while you cut them helps. I'm not sure why."

I'll have to put on my visor, I guess." I wiped the last of the tears from my eyes and squinted at Bean. She giggled quietly. I threw the chopped onion into the pan, where they sizzled angrily, the sound somehow struck me as satisfying.

10 / ASIMOV

> *Now, look, let's start with the three fundamental Rules
> of Robotics — the three rules that are built most deeply into
> a robot's positronic brain . . . one, a robot may not injure a
> human being or, through inaction, allow a human being to
> come to harm . . . Two, a robot must obey any orders given to
> it by human beings, except where such orders would conflict
> with the First Law . . . And three, a robot must protect its own
> existence as long as such protection does not conflict with the
> First or Second Law.*
>
> — Isaac Asimov, *Runaround*

I WAS WALKING the short way from the Saturday market to
the bus stop with Bean and Kate, who had come along for fun.
Dark clouds hung low in the sky, ready to hurl their contents on
top of us. It was nearly the end of the harvest season, and the
market would only be open for a few more weeks. I carried a few
bags on each arm, while Bean and Kate walked empty-handed.
They had offered to carry some of the load, but I told them that
I didn't feel the weight the same way they did. It didn't tire me,
then.

Just before we crossed the street to the bus stop, a teenage boy stepped out in front of us, seemingly from nowhere.

"Sabine," he spoke loudly. He smiled widely, but his eyes were not happy. His hair was shorn to his scalp.

"Oh," Bean breathed and walked closer to me, grabbing my arm. Kate muttered a few rude words under her breath and stepped closer, the two of us flanking Bean.

"What's this?" He glared at me and stepped in front of us as we attempted to walk around him.

"This is Alek. Alek, this is Jay. He's . . . he goes to my school."

"Hello," I said, and reached out a gloved hand. He shuddered, then stared at my hands. "Oh, I've heard about It. It's that robot that's got bioparts, huh? Creepy." He spoke more loudly as if I was deaf: "Hey Robofreak: you're cree-eepy." He elongated the word, so I could feel the syllables crawling up my back. He belched loudly.

"Gorillas make a belching sound as a sign of contentment," I said, realizing too late that this little tidbit would not help to diffuse the situation. Kate stifled a giggle.

"Are you calling me a gorilla?" Jay growled.

"Back off, Jay," Kate stepped forward, puffing out her body as threateningly as her small frame would allow.

"Hey Katie, keep practising the flute," Jay said, puckering his lips mockingly, "and you may just distract someone from your face long enough to get a boyfriend one day."

Bean stepped back and pulled me and Kate with her. "Be kind, Jay."

"What's behind the mask?" he growled, ignoring Bean and pointing at my visor.

"It's just more of my face," I spoke calmly, hiding my anxiety.

Without warning, Jay's hand shot out and grabbed my visor, ripping it from my face. Bean and Kate gasped as I blinked at him.

"Ugh," he stepped back, throwing the visor to the ground. "What the hell? Are those real?"

"That's enough, Jay," Bean's voice quavered.

"How can you be seen with this thing, yet you won't even let me take you to a concert."

"I'm not interested Jay," Bean's voice was a warning. Her fingers squeezed my unyielding arm.

"How many times does she have to tell you, Jay? Face it: you're a jerk." Jay glared at Kate then glanced over at me.

"Is he your robot boyfriend? Can't find a real guy who wants to date you?"

"Shut up, Jay." Tears glistened at the corners of her eyes. Jay moved to grab her. Kate squealed.

"That's enough," I said, stepping in front of Bean.

"Oh, it's a bodyguard?" He sneered. "Can you take a hit, Robofreak?"

"Jay, don't—" Bean was cut off as Jay reared back and delivered a solid punch to my jaw. I didn't feel it. Jay winced and rubbed his knuckles, realizing his mistake.

"Come on," he said, standing inches from me, "I've seen the news: I know you've got real hands under those gloves. What good are they if you don't use them for punching?" He stepped back and brought up his own fists, rocking on his heels.

I held up my hands in surrender. "I won't fight you. We just want to be on our way."

"Come on," Jay repeated, and before I could move, he delivered a swift kick to my left hand. I felt a crunch as pain shot into my hand. It was such a sudden and unexpected sensation that I dropped to my knees.

"Ah, a weak spot. Too bad it's your biobits." He savagely kicked my right hand with equal swiftness: another crunch and unbelievable pain. The bags I was holding slipped from my grasp. I folded up onto the pavement with my damaged hands, my head reeling. I heard a scream the second before Jay's full weight stomped down on both of my hands. Bean dropped down beside me and pulled my hands into her lap.

"Get out of here, Jay," she cried, tears glistening at the corners of her eyes.

"You freaks belong together," Jay looked down at us and laughed. As he walked away, he kicked at one of the bags lying on the sidewalk.

"Jerk!" Kate yelled in frustration and threw a pebble at his back. It bounced harmlessly off the pavement. I sat helplessly as Bean and Kate began gathering up any produce that hadn't rolled away. Kate picked up the bags as Bean pulled me to my feet.

We managed to get on the bus without too many stares. My hands sat brokenly in my lap. I felt numb all over except for the pulsing balls of pain attached to my arms. A few stops later, Kate stood up.

"This is my stop. Are you going to be okay?" she asked, looking from my hands to Bean's tear-streaked face.

"We're okay. I'll see you later." Kate took one last worried look at us before stepping off the bus. Bean began wiping synthetic blood away, gingerly probing the bruises that had already formed.

"Why didn't you hit him back?"

"I can't. It's one of Asimov's Three Laws of Robotics."

Asimov, the science fiction writer, wrote the Three Laws that would one day cross the boundaries from fantasy into reality and become standard programming for any SimAid.

My tone was bitter, something I had never before heard from my own voice. I was struck by the sensation as though, disconcertingly, I had two simultaneous, opposing thoughts existing in my consciousness. One belief was the unyielding rule that I could not harm a human. The other idea, more of a feeling, was that I wanted to hurt Jay very badly for how he had humiliated Bean.

"But I wanted to." I said minutes later, as we got off the bus.

"Wanted to what?"

"To hit him back. Hard. I wanted to slap the smug smile off his face. I wanted to break his hands." I paused. Bean's face was white, her eyes wide.

I continued. "But do you know what would happen to me if I ever struck a person? I would be returned to TARIA for termination." My voice was hard and jarring in my own ears.

"But, you're not a . . . a . . . " Bean's voice hitched at the unspoken word and tears flooded her eyes.

"Yet I still am, to everyone but you," I said cradling my broken hands as we walked back to the house.

"What happened?" Sebastien rushed over to us as we opened the front door.

Bean tried to speak, but was heaving with sobs and trying to catch her breath.

"Somebody named Jay thought it would be a good idea to try to beat me up," I answered.

"But why?"

"Apparently, he's never quite gotten over the fact that Bean turned him down for a date."

Sebastien looked over to Bean, who nodded, sniffling. He grabbed her arms. "Are you okay? Did he hurt you?"

"No, j-just Alek." She pointed at my hands. Sebastien looked down and realized how injured I was.

"This is not good," he said quickly. "Let's take you to the lab. Trent will be there; he practically lives at work."

"I'm coming." Bean spoke firmly. Her father didn't argue.

We hopped in the car and drove quickly over to TARIA. Despite that it was a weekend, cars dotted the parking lot and people came and went in the main lobby. We took the elevator down and walked the long, dimly lit hallway to Trent's lab.

Sebastien rapped once on the door and turned the handle. The door swung wide into the small room. In contrast to my last visit, the room looked dirty and unkempt as though Trent must have rarely left. A couch in the corner was partially covered in a dirt-stained blanket. Pizza boxes and bags of chips, empty burger wrappers and cups littered the floor. Tissues overflowed from a compost bin. Trent was in a back room of the lab, his back turned to us as we entered. When he heard the door shut, he wheeled around. He obviously had been told of our arrival; he didn't look surprised, but strode anxiously over to me and gently took hold of my hands. His skin felt clammy and cold. I wanted to pull away.

"What has happened? Tell me."

"Alek got into, uh, a fight," said Sebastien. I fought the urge to laugh at his explanation even though it didn't feel funny at all.

"Come, sit," Trent led me over to a low examination table, where I sat. He turned my hands over, prodding the bruised skin. "Tell me the story."

Bean told him of our run-in with Jay as Trent examined my hands.

"Can you bend your fingers?" As I bent my fingers gingerly, pain shot through my hands, fuzzily disappearing up my arm. Strangely, I felt tendrils of pain creep all the way up to my elbows.

"Both hands hurt."

"Good, that's good," Trent murmured, then, looking up and noticing the expressions on Bean and her father's faces, said quickly, "No, what I mean is, the nerve biosensor connection has not been severed. The pain means he's still receiving signals to his . . ." Trent's voice trailed off, as though deep in thought. He shook his head, and resumed speaking as if remembering he was not alone. "He seems to have a few broken fingers, but they should heal, just like his paper cut."

He began to splint my fingers. I kept wondering what he had been about to say about what was receiving my pain signals before he paused. I could tell that Sebastien was probably thinking the same thing; he kept looking at Trent curiously, then back at me, frowning, as if trying to figure out a puzzle for which the solution was hidden on my face.

Trent spoke as he wrapped gauze around my fingers, "Tell me, Alek, what did you feel when Jay hit you?"

Again with the testing. Bean glanced at me, the two of us thinking about the fortune teller's pronouncement of my connection to humanity. It was true; I felt it. But I still thought it was a dangerous confession to make to Adam Trent, my creator.

"A robot may not injure a human being or, through inaction, allow a human being to come to harm." I recited mechanically, covering my anger and fear.

"Explain."

"I could not let harm come to Sabine, but I could not directly harm Jay, either. I needed to distract him, take the hits, in a sense, that Sabine might have endured."

Trent stared at me, his expression unreadable.

"You were programmed to obey the Three Laws."

"Yes."

"At any point did you think of going against the Three Laws?"

"No." I lied. Yes, a lie. How was that possible? What purpose did a lie serve? I concluded that deceit was used as a form of self-preservation, spurred on by that overriding human emotion, base and instinctual: fear. I was not experiencing a programmed simulation of the appropriate response; this feeling was unbidden, uncontrolled.

Trent made a strangled sound and began to cough long, hacking coughs into a tissue he pulled from his lab coat pocket. Finally he spoke again.

"Do you feel more inclined to protect Sabine than, say, a stranger on the street?"

I carefully worded my answer. "I am in contact with Bean daily. I have more opportunities to look out for her well-being compared to the average citizen. If I saw that a stranger was in immediate danger, I would do what I could to try to help him or her."

"Yes, but what if you were given the choice? To protect Sabine or a stranger?"

I glanced at Bean, trying to hide my unease.

"I would protect Bean. She is part of the Archambault family. They are my primary responsibility."

Trent stared at me for a long time. I got the feeling he was looking for something beyond my metallic mask; he peered searchingly into my biological eyes.

I had nowhere to hide.

11 / ADVANCEMENT

A baby has brains, but it doesn't know much.
Experience is the only thing that brings knowledge,
and the longer you are on earth the more experience
you are sure to get.
– L. Frank Baum, *The Wonderful Wizard of Oz*

WHILE MY HANDS healed, I was practically useless around
the house. Ever since the incident with Jay, Bean's parents had
requested that I accompany her whenever she went out; but in
the house, I stood helplessly in my recharging dock, unable to
cook or clean since I could not use my hands to carry anything.
I could only answer the odd phone call. I began to feel antsy, anxious, bored, frustrated, useless. A useless SimAid isn't a SimAid
at all. I felt as though I was losing control. My mind wandered in
directions I had never intended it to go. I visualized possibilities I
had no right to even imagine. My emotional reactions to events
were exaggerated; I had to work hard to keep my feelings in check.

Eventually, Sebastien noticed my struggles. Catherine and
Bean had left early one morning—Catherine had a meeting with
a group of visiting nano experts and Bean had a string quartet

rehearsal. Sebastien had just come downstairs as I was attempting to dust the side tables in the living room. The dust cloth kept slipping from my hand since I couldn't grasp it adequately. I finally threw it down in frustration. I made a loud noise in disgust and didn't hear him until he entered the room. Looking up finally, I found him staring at me at me quizzically.

"Alek?" he spoke quietly. "Is everything all right?"

"I cannot serve the family the way I've been designed to. I . . ." I gave up trying to give the answers that were expected of me.

"I feel useless," I confessed. "It's very frustrating."

For the first time I had finally expressed my true emotions to someone other than Bean. Sebastien looked at me with less surprise than I would have expected. Somehow, he had suspected.

"Alek, I want you to come into work with me today."

"Why?" I asked. Worry crept into my voice; I couldn't help it.

"I want to run a few diagnostic tests on the uh, emotion program, that Trent installed. Since he's been off work sick, he can't do it himself."

"But I feel fine," I lied. My second lie ever.

"All the same," Sebastien quickly drained his cup of coffee and placed the empty mug in the sink. "I just want to see what's going on in that processor of yours."

We walked out the door and caught the next bus to the TARIA labs. I walked to the back of the bus and stepped into one of the SimAid charging docks lining the back row. Sebastien sat down on a free bench a few rows ahead. His head bent down and his fingers moved in blurs across the Intelli!pad he brought with him.

A few stops into the ride, a woman in a blue fur jacket with matching hair got on followed by a female-formed SimAid—it had softer edges, less angular than a male-formed model. It was a 3.2, an earlier version, I guessed by its lack of small upgrades similar to mine, such as bio-similar facial features and a coppery tone to the metallic skin. I turned to greet it, but the SimAid didn't look in my direction. It simply stepped up into the docking station. Its realistic face was blank and unmoving.

Several hours later, Sebastien sat down across from me. I had difficulty focussing on his face after having experienced several blackouts—I was uncertain of just how many—and having been scanned a dozen different ways in the diagnostics lab. His eyes reflected my own confusion.

"Something unexpected . . . has happened, or, uh, been done to you." He cleared his throat and looked down at his Intelli!pad, as if reading the answer but not quite understanding it. "You contain biological material that is, for lack of a better word, growing."

"My hands are growing?" I couldn't comprehend how that was possible.

"No, not your hands. Something in your head."

"My . . . brain?"

"Somebody has implanted what seem to be living cells into your processor. I can't tell you much more than that since the equipment in this lab can't be used to identify biological material. I don't quite know how or why, but I'm going to get to the bottom of this."

I was stunned. Now that I could finally feel, I felt numbly surprised. Sebastien stood quietly, but tensely waiting, as if expecting a large, physical reaction. I swallowed and asked simply, "Who did this?" I already knew the answer.

"I'm guessing Adam Trent knows something. That must be why he always acted so strangely whenever he visited us. He was so interested in you, in how you were functioning."

He picked up the Intelli!phone receiver—a private call—to prevent me from overhearing, and walked out into the hallway. I heard him mumbling. At times, his voice came out in a low hiss.

"Well, what did you think was going to happen? . . . he's feeling . . . I'm not going to . . . no, you're not coming up here . . . I need to think."

I heard Sebastien pacing the hall. He listened for a long time, then, he loudly said, "He's our business now, damn it!" He clicked off the phone brusquely and turned around.

He looked at me then, really looked at me. Not through the distorted lens of what his fuzzy expectations had formed in his mind but as though he finally saw me through his own human eyes. And I could tell that I wasn't what he expected; I was something new. My mind reeled, trying to figure out just what he had discovered.

"Alek," he spoke my name with great effort. "You are the result of a very ambitious and unethical man. Trent injected his own brain cells into your processor. He included neuroregenerative nanos whose job it was to break down the mechanical systems of your program to make room and provide nutrients and information for the biological bits to grow and multiply. Essentially, the brain cells gradually took over the functioning for your electronic computer chip of a memory. At the end of the process, you will have an entirely human brain occupying a mechanical body."

"Yes." I said. That one word was all I could manage. In truth, how could I even understand the difference? I had felt the slow transformation of my ideas, the growth of my emotions, the development of my attitudes.

"What am I?" I whispered, but I didn't want an answer. I just wanted him to think about the enormity of it. He turned away, a white lab-coated back.

I had to go. I wanted to hear it from Adam Trent. I wanted him to explain me what he had done, why he had done it. However, I couldn't leave without permission. No SimAid had ever had an independent thought outside of what was instructed of it. Despite my desire to see Trent, I still needed permission. I belonged to the Archambault family, and I knew that nothing would get me deactivated more quickly than if I started acting of my own free will. I needed Bean's help. But what would I tell her? I didn't know how to begin. Sebastien and I left the building in silence and rode the bus back to the Archambault home.

12 / AMBITION

Pay no attention to the man behind the curtain!
– L. Frank Baum, *The Wonderful Wizard of Oz*

BEAN WAS IN her room practising the cello. I had learned to tell from her choice of music what kind of mood she was in. The quick, staccato way in which she played high and scratchy notes told me that Bean was angry with something or someone. I knocked on her door. The sounds of cello abuse stopped.

"What?" She shouted.

"May I come in?"

A pause, and then, "Yes."

I walked into the bedroom. Bean sat in the corner at her music stand with her bow and cello still in her hands.

"I need you to come with me to see Adam Trent," I began.

"Is he doing a diagnostic? I thought you'd already had that done. Is there something wrong?" Bean spoke anxiously.

"Nothing. Nothing is wrong, really," I said. "Your father took me over to TARIA today to do some tests."

"Then what is going on?"

I didn't want to tell her. She wouldn't be able to trust me now that I wasn't a machine, wasn't human. She'd think I was a monster.

But one look at the expression of concern on Bean's face convinced me that I could confide in her. "My brain is . . . has transformed."

"Like a virus? Into what?"

"I guess it's like a virus. It's . . . human. My brain, I mean, is made up of human brain cells."

She set her bow and cello down on the ground. Her mouth hung open to form a new question, but she seemed unsure what to ask next.

"I don't understand. How could . . . Why? I mean, have you always had a human brain then?"

"No, that's the really exceptional part. My human biological brain cells divided and grew and eventually replaced my programming chips."

Bean stood up then, and walked over to me. She stood within arm's length, looking up at me. She reached out and touched the middle of my forehead, just above my eyes.

"Here. You are human."

"Am I?"

"Yes. I felt it somehow. That market day when we visited the fortune teller's booth. She was right." As Bean took a deep breath and slowly let it out, I felt my worries about her acceptance of me flow out of my body. "And now you want an explanation," she added simply.

"Yes."

"Let's go."

I had gathered from Sebastien's phone conversation that Trent must still be somewhere in TARIA. Before entering the main reception area, I leaned over to Bean.

"You know you have to do the talking."

"Yes. Out in public, everyone considers you to be my SimAid chaperone. How strange, considering I'm here to support you!" She giggled nervously.

The sliding doors glided soundlessly in front of us. The visitors' desk was quiet. The receptionist behind the glass slowly flipped the pages of an Intelli!reader with the listlessness of someone who's not really seeing the words on the screen. She noticed me first, her eyes widening with alarm to see a SimAid without accompaniment. Her eyes then slid over to Bean who stood to my left and a little behind me. She took in Bean's layers of oddly matched clothing and large boots.

"Yes?"

"We're here to see Adam Trent." Bean told her.

"Do you have an appointment?" She spoke in a monotone, betraying boredom.

"No, but he'll want to see us. Could you please tell him Sabine Archambault is here with Alek?"

The receptionist stared at Bean for a moment, then pressed a button on her earpiece. "Adam Trent." She paused. "Yes, Dr. Trent, a Sabine Archambault accompanied by a SimAid would like to see you."

"Alek," Bean corrected her. The woman appeared not to hear her. She listened for a moment, then looked surprised and said, "Yes, I will send them down."

She pressed a button again on her earpiece then said, "Fourth floor, lab room 473. The elevator is down that hall to the left," her hand waved vaguely in the direction of the hall.

"Thank you." Bean grabbed my arm. "Come on."

We took the elevator to the fourth floor, then walked down a long hall, past endless doors, from behind which came strange, yet eerily familiar sounds. Finally, we stood in the doorway of lab 473. The door swung open.

"My, my, Sabine and her SimAid. What a pleasure it is to see you." Bean and I both nodded but said nothing.

"How you've grown since I first met you. Both of you," Adam Trent added, looking at me but speaking to Sabine. He smiled broadly with his mouth, yet his eyes looked hard. Something had changed; he looked thinner, more pale.

"I'll wait over there," Bean said to me, motioning to a bench just down the hall. I nodded. We both watched her walk away. Trent closed the door. Had I lungs, I would have taken a deep breath.

"Dr. Trent."

He took a breath as if to speak, but dissolved into a fit of coughing. I waited. "Alek, you always preferred that name to your model, didn't you?" he croaked.

"Yes." I answered flatly. There was no use hiding the truth any longer.

"And so," he paused taking a ragged breath. His voice sounded differently than it had in the past: hoarse, weaker. "The real question is, how are you feeling?"

"Fearful. Confused. Overjoyed. Hopeful. Shall I go on?"

"So you've been hiding some things from me."

"I have. I don't know why, but I didn't want to . . . couldn't . . . tell you how I was changing."

"You've become exactly how I had hoped you'd turn out."

"Why?"

A look in his eyes, like a lion tracking its prey, renewed my fear. I knew then that I'd hear only half truths at best.

"Why not?" Trent searched my face, as if my human-made parts could fully express the range of emotion I felt in my head.

"Am I an experiment for a new model of SimAid? If so, I have to protest that it's rather cruel."

"No. Not another SimAid. A simulated human."

"Not a real one?"

"I don't know, Alek. Do you feel real like a real boy?" He spoke teasingly.

"So I'm just a toy, a puppet, then? If I'm Pinocchio, I guess that makes you Gepetto."

"You've been reading a lot, I take it," Trent's chuckle turned into another long, hacking cough. He turned away for a moment with a tissue held to his mouth. I noticed spots of blood before he squirrelled it away into his pocket.

"Are you ill?"

"It's nothing. Simply my humanity betraying me." He wiped his forehead then turned to face me again. "Just think of the possibilities for humans, Alek! Brain damage can be reversed. Brain dysfunction can be repaired. I'll be a legend in the field of neuroscience!"

"And me? What will I be?"

"A textbook chapter. Hell, an entire volume!"

"I see." The fear heightened. "What now?"

"What do you want, Alek?"

"I want . . ." I stopped.

What did I want?

"I want to be accepted. I want to be human." I waited for him to laugh, but he didn't. He looked at me triumphantly.

"Exactly. Of course you do."

"I want a human body. Can you do that?"

Trent looked at me for what seemed like a lifetime. He tilted his head, taking me in. His darkly shadowed eyes flitted back and forth, as if making some internal calculations.

"Yes. You shall be human. Fully."

"How?"

"We will grow you a body. Stem cell research has advanced exponentially, you know. We will transplant some of the more complicated organs. You will look human, feel human."

"Will I be human?"

"Ah, now that will be for you to determine."

"Is it? Is it really up to me?"

Trent's eyes resumed their predatory look. "You and I both know that according to the law, you are still the property of the Archambault family . . . for now. Let's just call it an experiment and leave it at that for the moment."

"Will the Archambaults agree?"

"Catherine has been with me for every step of this new, uh, evolution in robotics. She'll support me without a doubt. Of course, I will need assistance from both human surgeons and robotic engineers in the multiple procedures that you will have to undergo, but I will certainly be overseeing and keeping close watch. After all, you're my own . . . uh, design."

Did I have a choice? Was it even my decision to make? Though I brought up the desire to become fully biological, I got the feeling that it had been Trent's plan all along. But the thought of looking and feeling fully human excited me. I would no longer be a freak, an anomaly of nature and invention.

Would I?

How does it feel to have a human brain and a mechanical body? No different, I supposed, than having a human brain and a biological body. In both cases, the brain is a control centre occupying a small space in a larger vehicle. However, human identity seems to be closely related to—and often dependent on—physical appearance. Just as an amputee might have difficulty considering a new robotic limb as a part of himself or herself, it was a challenge for a biological brain to self-identify with a mechanical body. Somehow this awareness made me feel turned inside out. I needed my outsides to match my insides.

I tried to explain it all, including Trent's plans for me, to Bean as we walked back through the hospital and out into the dull, overcast day.

Bean stopped and put a hand on my arm. "Isn't that what everyone wants, Alek? For people to see us—to really see us—for who we are? You're no different from anyone else in that respect."

Of course Bean would consider me just like everyone else. Some human part of me glowed warmly from her comment.

"It's one thing to look beyond scars or a dirty face. But to look beyond this?" I touched my hard unreadable face. Bean reached up to pull my hand away from my face. She gave it a squeeze.

"I see you," she said.

At her words, something sparked inside me, a random memory from one of my many sessions of Intelli!net information gorging, back when I was still connected.

Back before I was me.

"*Sawubona*," I murmured.

"Pardon?"

"*Sawubona*. It means 'I see you.' It's how you greet someone in Zulu. The Zulus define a person by their connection to another. The reply is *Ngikhona*, meaning 'I am here'."

Bean shook her head and smiled. "Your human brain never ceases to surprise me."

Despite our conversation, the fearful nagging feeling that something was not quite right kept me distracted, I didn't speak to Bean on our way out of the building or as we waited for the bus. Bean didn't try to speak to me.

As the bus pulled up and we got on, I took up my usual spot in the charging docks at the back of the bus. Bean stopped in front of me, but turned around so that we stood silently face-to-face; we tended to draw attention if people overhead us engaging in conversation.

The bus stopped and a male-formed SimAid 3.3 got on. It walked to the back and stepped onto the charging dock beside me. Its biological features were eerily similar to mine. Just as most families personalized their Intelli!pads with unique skins and functions, they similarly customized their SimAids. This one had slightly larger eyes and a bright yellow stripe across the top of its head. I glanced first at my own hands and then at the SimAid's factory model appendages. It looked straight ahead, as if awaiting instruction. Was that what I was once like? Could anyone tell outwardly that I was different? As I stood there, mechanically, awkwardly, Bean reached over and patted my arm.

"It's okay," she spoke quietly. "It's not you. You're not the same as it."

I saw that she was right. I had no more in common with this being than I would with an electric can opener. I felt no kinship to this thing. It was fully mechanical. It didn't contain a single biological cell within its factory-made shell. Nonetheless, as we both stood, patiently waiting for our stop, I felt awkward, as if I were in the same room with a distant relative with whom I had nothing to talk about.

13 / ALTERNATIVES

I FILLED MY days with work, concentrating on each dust mote I swept, every pinch of spice that went into a soup, any overgrown weeds to be pulled from the gardens. The worrying and wondering part of my brain worked somewhere in the background. I imagined it was like this for everyone. Anticipating a university acceptance, waiting on a cancer diagnosis, expecting a baby, while continuing with everyday life—humans turn robot-like when consumed by unanswered questions.

One evening, after Catherine and Sebastien had gone out, Bean and I cleaned the kitchen. She had begun helping me with chores, but only when her parents weren't home.

"Why do you do the work I'm supposed to be doing?" I asked her as I cleaned the table with a damp cloth. Bean looked up from a dish she was washing.

"My parents never expected me to have chores of my own. You've done everything. It makes me feel uncomfortable, strange, to see you working so hard all the time."

"Did it always? Make you feel so uncomfortable, I mean?"

"No," she admitted. "But I was young when you came. I just expected people to clean up after me. It didn't matter if they were human or . . . what."

I was the What.

"What am I to you?" I asked. We stood quietly now, facing each other.

"You are . . . you've always been . . . Alek to me." She reached out and touched my hand. "If this is what makes you feel more like Alek, then you need to get the operation."

"What if I'm different? What if I'm no longer . . . me?" The visor that normally hid my human eyes was tilted up on my head. I held her eyes in mine, searching for answers. Bean looked back at me, eyes wide and unblinking. A small crease appeared between them.

"What's the alternative? To stay this way, You and Not-Quite-You, forever?"

I felt overwhelmed. What did I want? How did I end up on this path? What if the operations couldn't make me human? Could I accept the half-human I had become?

Despite my inhuman features, Bean somehow recognized my panic. She squeezed my hand still held under hers.

"You'll be okay, Alek."

Yet I could hear the uncertainty and fear in her voice mirroring my own.

An appointment was set for early December. I had convinced

myself that it had been my own choice, my decision; but of course, by now I had learned the subtle art of lying to myself.

Sebastien, Catherine, and I sat in a row of chairs in the office of one of TARIA's medical buildings. Bean had insisted on joining us; her parents only agreed when she argued that she wanted to sit in to gain insight for her independent science project, "Mechanical vs. Genetically-Engineered Transplantation."

We had arrived several minutes earlier to the hospital-like building, a two-story structure housing many of the experimental medical procedures that TARIA had pioneered. Those who expressed vocal opposition to humans being used as TARIA's guinea pigs—albeit consensually—called it Dr. Frankenstein's Laboratory. A sign above the reception desk informed me that we were in the Implants/Transplants wing. We were escorted immediately to a small office down the hall.

I stared down at my fingers, wiggling them one at a time, then all together. Sebastien read the news scrolling across the Intelli!screen. Catherine sat typing on her Intelli!pad. Bean looked over to me and smiled nervously.

A tall and energetic woman bounced into the room. She shook hands with the Archambaults, her bluntly cut black hair swishing around her face.

"I'm Dr. Pam, chief surgeon here at TARIA medical labs," she said, sitting down behind her desk. "I'll be overseeing your various surgeries. I'm sure you have questions." She looked at all of us, her dark eyes as piercing and probing as the tools of her profession; I felt as though the comment was directed primarily at me. She obviously knew my history, knew I felt human.

"How long will the procedures take?" Catherine asked.

"The total surgery time should take somewhere between sixty and seventy hours, but the recovery between transplants and after full biological transference will add months. It will take upwards of six months before Alek will be able to stay conscious for a normal period of time."

"How certain are you that this biological transference will work?" Sebastien glanced sideways at me.

"You have to remember that none of these procedures are new or revolutionary. We've been replacing human parts with lab-grown bits for a few decades now. Alek's situation is unusual because he will essentially be replacing his entire system almost all at once."

As I listened to Dr. Pam talk on about integrated wetware, gradual release of electronic systems, and vital organs working towards complete autonomy, I felt even less like a person than I did when I had walked into the office. Dr. Pam must have noticed the expression on my face, because in the middle of explaining the process of imprinting skin tissue she stopped and turned fully, looking only at me.

"Do my explanations make you feel uneasy, Alek?"

"Oh, I doubt if he even understands completely what is going on," Catherine jumped in.

"Of course he does!" Bean came quickly to my defence. "Don't forget that he's got a fully human brain, Mother. He thinks and feels just like us."

I could see Catherine bristling at her daughter's last comment.

She sat up straighter in her chair, looking from Bean's face to my own.

"I do feel anxiety at the thought of so many procedures," I admitted to Dr. Pam. "Will I be aware?"

"You will be sedated for most of the process, and kept in a medically induced coma throughout the healing. No one is certain of the amount of pain you will experience. Your neurons will be busily creating pathways, and we won't know for sure if they're sending complete signals from your brain to your body and vice versa until we bring you back to consciousness."

After Dr. Pam completed her explanation of the various procedures, she paused and took a deep breath. "I know this is a lot to process," she looked not only at Catherine and Sebastien, but also at me. "But now, the fun part. You essentially get to build yourself. I'm going to leave this up to Alek, since he has to live with it." The doctor spoke quickly as she noticed Catherine beginning to open her mouth in protest.

Dr. Pam turned to me and handed over an Intelli!pad with CGI body parts to scroll through.

"Choose your face," she said, smiling.

I looked up. "Pardon me?"

"Look through these pictures of sample faces and cranial structures. Let me know which one seems most like you."

I thought for a moment. I didn't look at myself regularly. I needed help from someone who really saw me.

"Can I have help?"

"Of course."

I turned to Bean, who sat in the chair beside me. While Sebastien and Catherine discussed with Dr. Pam the finer details of the operations, Bean and I began playing around with a cranial mapping program; essentially, we began creating my face from scratch, pulling bits and pieces from the side menus: this eyebrow ridge, this nose, this jaw, these ears.

After a few moments of dragging various facial features and bone structures onto the blank template, I sat back.

"How about this one?"

Bean leaned towards the screen and squinted. "No, the face is too thin."

"How about . . . this one?" I said after making a few more changes. Bean scowled.

"Too movie star-ish."

Bean changed the hairline, made the ears slightly larger, widened the ocular cavities. I felt as though she had just fit together the last piece of a puzzle. Something about the face looked familiar.

It looked like home.

"Yes."

Bean smiled up at me. "Perfect."

Hours later, I fully understood the concept of mental exhaustion. There were too many choices. I was asked to choose my height, build, skin and hair colour. When they started in on the size and shape of my feet, Sebastien began to laugh.

"This feels exactly like when we were custom building our house," he said, looking to Catherine. "We had to choose everything: living space size, where to put Intelli!screens, wall colour, tile styles. It's overwhelming." He patted me on the shoulder.

"I had the most difficult decision after narrowing the kitchen backsplash down to two kinds of tile," Catherine added.

"I had to hide both samples behind my back while you chose a hand, remember?" Sebastien grinned at his wife. Catherine's normally tight-lipped smile loosened slightly at the memory.

"Make me look average," I told them. "I just want to pass for human."

"You won't have to pass," Dr. Pam spoke softly. "You will be."

And so began a countless parade of doctors, neuro-scientists, and nano technicians, each with their own vested interest in my transformation. My hands were poked and prodded, my brain was scanned and probed, my bot-body was tested and surveyed. Everyone talked over me but never directly to me, unless asking for a response to a question about my functioning. I felt for the first time in a long time more like my old SimAid self. Only when Dr. Pam came to see me did I feel noticed. She oversaw most of the planning and operations: a complex choreography of specialized teams responsible for the various surgeries, or upgrades, as they often referred to them.

I was a miracle in the making: a new species to some, a unique experiment in bio-technology to others.

"Teach me to dance."

I stood in the doorway to Bean's room. She had been doing homework at her desk. The music that typically accompanied her work thumped out of hidden wall speakers. I had just brought up an after-school snack, a plate of carrots and peanut dip, which she had finished off in record time.

Bean started laughing until she realized how sincere I was.

"Now? Your surgery starts tomorrow. Why not after, when you've recovered?"

"What if . . . what if there is no after?" There. I'd said it. The worry had bubbled over and out into words that I had only ever thought and never said aloud.

"What do you mean?" Bean's brows furrowed.

"What if something goes wrong? What if my various parts reject each other? What if my memories or my entire mind is destroyed in the process?" I paused. "What if it's just not possible?"

Bean stood and stared at me. As she searched my eyes, I saw all of my worry reflected in her own large, green eyes, as if she had been having the same thoughts.

Bean reached over and touched the Intelli!screen. The thumping of heavy bass was replaced by a softer beat. My brain stilled as I listened to the slowly growing sound. Bean took my hands and placed them around her waist.

"Close your eyes and listen," she said, her eyes already shut.

I couldn't close my eyes. I needed to register with both my existing human senses: touch and sight. I looked down at Bean's face; her long lashes resting just above her cheeks, the muscles slowly easing around her eyes and mouth. Her body began to sway slightly and I fell into the rhythm with her. I could feel the cool fabric of the shirt that hung at her waist and beneath it, the soft give of her skin, the slight movements of the muscles as she rolled her hips in time to the music. I moved with her, imitating her rhythmic swaying. I felt the sound overtake me, infiltrating me, and I became conscious of the difference in sensations between the real parts of me and those that were mechanical. My body vibrated numbly. I could control it, sense that it was there, but it wasn't really a part of me. The music rose in volume and intensity. As I let it flood through me, I concentrated again on Bean's face. A single tear had escaped beneath her closed eyelids and trickled down her cheek. I reached over and touched it, rubbing the wetness between two fingers. I wanted to laugh, cry, yell. I wanted to run, pound the wall, stay here holding Bean forever. I wanted to do so many things that my body could not yet do.

I felt as though something inside me wanted out.

14 / AGONY

*Nothing is so painful to the mind as a great and
sudden change.*
– Mary Shelley, *Frankenstein*

SO THIS IS PAIN, is my first groggy thought upon awakening.
Pain pulls you into the present like nothing else; it is a torturous
meditation. There is no future, no memory, only the pain.

I feel like a science project. I am a strange, unidentifiable
Thing crumpled at the bottom of a jar, grown out of adolescent
curiosity. While my new body settles in, a thin barrier of plastic
film framing my bed protects me from the various microscopic
organisms that could shake apart the fragility of my new shell.

I am kept in standby mode, or a medically induced coma,
depending on the phase of my transformation, for six months.
In that time, biological systems have developed alongside, then
replaced, my circuitry. Fragile living cells overlap impermeable
super-alloy materials. I am Superman becoming mere Man.

Nerve endings, raw and exposed, shoot electrical impulses up the tree of bundled fibres like an early warning system: Caution . . . Danger . . . letting me know that something is not quite right. The agony makes me restless. I find it impossible to lie in one place. As I move, my body screams out from a new and different place of pain. I am a ball of red- and white-hot light. I am nothing but the pain. I feel as though if this sensation stopped, I would cease to exist altogether.

A nurse enters the room. She sees me writhing at the bottom of my plastic container. Her hands do something upon which I can't concentrate. The white heat fades to grey . . . then black . . . then nothing . . .

My breath is rhythmically pumped into me then wrenched away. Eventually, my lungs become strong enough to labour on their own. It hurts to breathe—but I breathe! I am an entire Halloween skeleton grown from a Petri dish of bone cells, forced into differentiation. I am a child's song: "the knee bone connected to the thigh bone, the thigh bone connected to the hip bone."

My skin has been similarly grown and grafted into place in squares of raw nerve endings. Luckily, I am unconscious for weeks on end as I am patched together, and am only pulled from my induced coma once the majority of the healing has taken place and the pain, though all-encompassing, is at a tolerable level.

I had no way of calculating how much time had passed. My new life had begun early in the New Year as a series of disconnected sights, sounds, and sensations. I remembered nurses and doctors costumed in what looked like radiation suits working as a team, gingerly rotating my body to remove old bandages and replace them with new ones. Various tubes and bags were periodically attached and detached from my orifices.

Sebastien and Catherine came in occasionally to make notes, take photos, speak with doctors. I don't remember seeing Adam Trent; later, when I was more fully conscious, I thought his absence seemed strange.

Yet all along, there was Bean.

Bean's face floated, fuzzy and distorted behind the thin membrane. Some days she sat in a chair at the far corner of the room, where I could barely tell that she was there. Other days, she stood so closely that I could see her breath on the plastic partition. Once or twice I remember hearing the soothing sounds of her cello, but I couldn't turn my head to see her. Another time she had brought a book and read aloud to me. Despite the red strips of pain that blinded my eyes and deafened my ears, her voice floated through the agony, like a cooling mist to dampen the fire in my head.

Bit by bit, the torturous tidal waves that threatened to overtake me slowly began to recede. I could move my head towards the sounds that the nurses and doctors made when they came into the room. I began to hear the constant, reassuring beat of a ticking clock, marking off each second that led towards my recovery.

Once I tried to move my head enough to look at my body, but I was bandaged from head to toe and could only make out white wrappings, oozing red, brown, and yellow in spots. I tried to lift my hands to my face. I felt as though I was lifting hundred-pound weights, as my hands slowly appeared before my eyes, whole and human, wrists ending in more bandages. I wiggled each finger in turn. They obeyed reluctantly, like miniature martial arts students bowing before their Sensei. The sight of my hands, still whole and attached, comforted me. I placed palm to palm; my sense of touch had been somewhat deadened, for all I could feel was the pins-and-needles prickle of pinched nerves.

Another moment stands out, a memory, I think: it was near the end of my medically induced coma, when I was almost done the majority of my healing. The wrappings around my head had been removed. I remember the new sensation of cool air tickling my cheeks. Something must have awoken me, a presence in the room, a noise. I opened my eyes to Catherine standing over me. She had the most conflicted expression on her face, as though multiple feelings were battling inside her. Even in my groggy state, I could still perceive the micro-emotions flitting across her face like storm clouds punctuated by brief moments of sunlight. One moment she gazed at me with a look of tenderness, as one would look at a child. The next, she seemed confused, trying to make sense of the human face she was now seeing. Then her eyes darkened and narrowed as if refusing to accept what was in front of her; a startled gasp rattled out of her as she finally noticed my eyes opening, and she hurried from the room.

Human beings rely so much on their sense of sight and hearing but often forget about the sense of smell. What a rare and beautiful gift to be able to identify such subtleties! How inextricably linked are these scents to our memory: To be able to pinpoint the exact moment when the cookies baking in the oven are done; to suddenly recall the name of the girl who sat behind you in grade 10 History when someone else walks by with her perfume; to recognize the familiar scent of your own house when you return home after a long holiday. Before my transformation, a sense of smell and taste was simply a matter of detecting and identifying minute molecules of substances wafting through the air. Now I understood how strongly smell is tied to memory.

My first smell after recovering from my operation was the scent of coconut; the nurse who tended to my bandages had soft hands, moisturized with a lightly scented lotion. The sweet milk-iness of coconut doesn't bring to my mind a tropical getaway, but a hospital stay full of physical pain, softly probing hands, and sound without sight. The scent will forever bring me back to those months.

Months/moments/days/hours later, a doctor stood at the side of my bubble and spoke directly to me, as if expecting a response. It was the first time anyone had tried to communicate directly with me, rather than simply speaking to fill up the silent space that surrounded a comatose patient.

"It's Doctor Pam," she said. "How are you feeling?"

"'M feelin'," someone croaked. With sudden alarm, I sensed that a stranger had stolen my words and was speaking for me!

"Your larynx needs to be worked in slowly," Dr. Pam reassured me. "It's never been used. Give it time. Can you whisper?"

"How does one whisper?" The strange voice croaked again.

"Form the words with your mouth, lips and tongue, and push out air from your lungs, but don't try to use your voice box." I tried to visualize her instructions.

"Li' dis?" I hissed. It felt strange to use muscles to form words. I needed practice. Luckily I seemed to have learned subconsciously the ways in which people formed sounds by watching them speak. I had to think about what my mouth was doing, but I was able to produce the suggestion of words. My throat and mouth felt dry and sticky. I experimented by moving my tongue around inside my mouth, which helped a little bit.

"Yes, that's great," Dr. Pam sounded pleased. "I'm surprised that you're able to make any sounds at all. How is your pain level?"

"Nottin' to cmper it to," I whispered.

"The fact that you are conscious and are able to answer my questions means that the pain can't be unbearable. That's good. I'll keep your morphine drip, but reduce the levels slightly and see how you do. She fiddled with a bag near my bed.

"If your white blood count looks good, we can take down the barrier," she said, flicking at the plastic walls surrounding me. "That will simplify things somewhat. All your major systems seem to have kicked in and are working well. We had a few false starts for a while there, but you're running like a well-oiled machine now—or, er, human."

I tried to smile. "'M all bi-logical?"

Dr. Pam smiled warmly. "Hurts to be human, doesn't it?"

"Hands c'n't feel." I tried to explain, lifting them off the bed.

"That's quite normal. Your nervous system is still working out all its pathways and the signals aren't always making it to their destination. The human body is an amazing machine, Alek. It is still working at repairing itself."

That was one thing my SimAid body could never have done.

I abruptly felt a heavy weight on my eyelids and throughout my entire body.

"You need to rest," I heard Dr. Pam say as I drifted off. "It's exhausting to adjust to an entirely new body."

Adam Trent remained conspicuously absent for the duration of my recovery. It made me uneasy, but at the same time, his absence helped me feel less like his own personal experiment and more like a real human recovering from life-changing surgery.

I was abruptly awake. Two women's voices floated just beyond the curtain surrounding my bed. One was Dr. Pam, ever-present in my waking and half-conscious moments. I quickly identified the other voice by the conversation.

"What is Alek's purpose?" Dr. Pam spoke in low tones.

"What do you mean?" Catherine's voice was just as quiet, but with an edge.

"He's human now, you must realize that."

"Of course. Biologically speaking."

"There is no difference. He may have not started out the same way the rest of us did, but in my professional opinion, he's human."

"It's a good thing no one is asking for your professional opinion, then. As far as we are concerned, he belongs to us and will continue to work for us."

"Is that what Alek wants?"

"What Alek wants doesn't have any bearing on the situation. You have been hired to oversee his surgeries—for a great deal of money, I might add—and we are not interested in your musings about his humanity. Alek is all about the advancement of humanity."

"What do you mean by that?"

"Is it credit you want? Don't worry, my dear doctor. When this is all over, your name will be included with the others when people generations from now talk about our pioneering advancement of human life."

Days passed slowly in the recovery wing. At first, I was comforted by the routine, by the same faces visiting me day after day, but then I grew bored, restless for my release.

I awoke early each morning to a nurse in colourful animal-patterned scrubs pulling open the curtains. She'd set my breakfast tray in my lap and sit down beside me, talking the entire time I ate my meal. I learned that her name was Cindy, and that she lived on her own with two cats, a dog, and a bearded dragon. She biked to and from work. On really awful days, she took the bus. Cindy was pleasant enough, but clearly was nervous around me. She never questioned me other than "How are you feeling," never referred to me by name. She didn't need to call me by name, of course, since I was the only other person in the room; however, by not using my name, I felt as though she was keeping a safe distance from me.

Cindy clearly had no idea what to ask me about my strange and unique new life. Instead, she filled the void with random details about herself. She liked playing Scrabble. She had a mother with Alzheimer's who refused treatment and was wasting away in a nursing home. She met with friends for dinner at the restaurant across the street every Friday. She collected silver rings, but wasn't allowed to wear them on the job.

Once Cindy left with the empty breakfast tray, I turned on the Intelli!screen in my room and watched random clips of news events around the world. I was appalled, as always, by what people considered to be newsworthy. Most items discussed were sensationalist and negative. I was surprised that I hadn't heard of my own operation, but realized that due to its experimental and rather controversial nature, my transformation had been kept quiet.

Mick, the quiet and burly physiotherapist typically made his entrance late morning, just as I was being lulled into half-sleep by the newscasters' voices. Luckily, Mick's arms were twice as thick as my rarely used legs. For the first several weeks, he had to physically remove me from the bed and place me in a wheelchair before pushing me to the physio room, or the torture chamber as many of its victims referred to it.

Mick didn't engage in polite conversation while he pushed my body to its limits; he encouraged me with slow nods and shoulder squeezes with his tough, bear paw hands. Occasionally he would say, "Good job." He never apologized for the pain he inflicted on me.

After the two hours, I'd be sweaty, sore, exhausted. Mick would lower me back into my wheelchair and wheel me into the hydrotherapy room, where my muscles would be soothed by warm jets of water. When the jets were turned off, I'd suck in a breath and lower myself completely under the water. I'd let my arms and legs go, and they'd float and sway slightly just below the surface. I'd imagine that my body was cradled in a giant womb, surrounded by embryonic fluid; I'd envision myself as the infant that my strangely evolved existence never had the chance to experience. My mind would shut off, and I'd feel contentedly blissful. Half an hour later, Mick would lift me out and help me towel off.

The afternoon would consist of lunch, nap, and doctor visits. Some days, Sebastien and Catherine came in together; other times, Catherine came alone. Sabine was rarely allowed to accompany her parents, but she sometimes made the trip in secret, often bringing me new and wonderful food for my emerging taste buds to experience, and playing whatever new piece she had practiced on her cello. Trent was always strangely absent. Catherine maintained that she was taking notes for him. He was avoiding the press, she told me, who had been tipped off to my existence by unscrupulous TARIA insiders. Adam Trent, a highly recognizable face of TARIA, would give away my presence if he visited.

A few months into my recovery, on a particularly good day when I felt strong, rested, and optimistic, Bean showed up with chocolate and a bag of potato chips. I hadn't yet tried chocolate, but chips and their salty, satisfying crunch were my favourite of the foods that Bean had snuck in so far. I had already sampled such delicacies as black liquorice and sour keys, often accompanied by a new book or Bean's portable chessboard.

As I tore into the bag of salt-and-vinegar chips, mumbling my thanks over a mouthful, Bean sat on the edge of the bed recounting the latest exploits of Russell and Shawn.

"And they say 'hi' and hope you're feeling nothing like your old self," she said. I smiled through a mouthful of chips.

"Ha. Ha." I put another chip experimentally on my tongue until the sharpness of the vinegar curiously made my eyes water. Bean stopped talking for a moment and simply watched me.

"What?" I said, feeling self-conscious. Bean smiled.

"Nothing, I just look at you and I . . . I can't imagine you any other way. It's like your old body was a cocoon, and you've finally emerged as—"

"As a butterfly?" I said, spraying crumbs over the bed.

"No," Bean laughed, "As you."

"You know I wasn't always like this. I started off just like all the other SimAids."

"I know," Bean frowned. "I was younger. You were like a fabulous toy come to life; the perfect playmate. You've evolved into so much more, though. Alek, you're real to me now."

"An imaginary friend turned real?" I teased.

"More." Her eyes scanned my face, searching. "Alek, I—"

Just then, Sebastien and Catherine came in.

"What on earth —" Catherine started.

"Oh, hi!" Bean popped up off the bed, her face pink. The chip bag fell to the ground, spilling the remains of its contents. I was just trying to help Alek develop his sense of taste."

"With potato chips?" Sebastien's eyebrows raised and he hid a smile on his face while he bent down to pick up the bag.

"And chocolate?" Bean's mother took the bar from the night table, frowning. "You know Alek is on a strict diet while his digestive system grows accustomed to different foods."

"It's okay, Mother, the nurses know that when I'm here I bring—" she stopped, realizing she'd given away too much. Catherine stared at her daughter as if trying to make sense out of an abstract painting.

"Wait a minute. You've done this before? More than once?"

"Well, yeah, sometimes after school I take the bus."

"You don't need to be here. This is not your concern."

"Of course it is. Alek's been in my life for the past seven years, Mother, I—"

"I don't want to hear any more. I will speak to the hospital staff about this. If I hear that you've been coming alone to see him, I will forbid you from joining us on our visits."

Finally, Sebastien spoke up.

"Catherine, I don't think it's a big concern. Obviously the doctors and nurses didn't think a little junk food was damaging to Alek." Catherine whirled on him, clutching the chocolate bar so hard that it snapped.

"I'd expect you of all people to understand. She's a teenage girl and should be doing teenage things. Not interfering with a scientific breakthrough. It's just not . . . not . . . appropriate!" She spat the final word out.

Sebastien stood still, stunned. Bean remained equally still, looking down at the floor. I was on the verge of comprehension, but couldn't quite grasp what the conversation was really about. Even with my newly developing understanding of human response, I knew Catherine's was an overreaction.

The family left quickly, Bean casting a quick look of apology and mouthing, "See you later," over her shoulder.

I didn't see Bean again for a month, and only accompanied by her parents. The nurses were sympathetic. They clearly missed her presence, but didn't dare go against Catherine's orders.

I concentrated my thoughts on healing, on becoming whole.

My legs still shorted out from time to time, the nerves still trying to fix a path from my body to my brain. Occasionally, I still had trouble recognizing my various body parts as belonging to me, and felt as if they were attached to someone else. This condition, Dr. Pam explained, was known as depersonalization. It occurred sometimes with traumatic head injuries. My mind was experiencing a massive identity crisis, not yet having associated the body attached to it as part of itself. A large part of physiotherapy with Mick was not only strengthening my new muscles, but getting my brain to accept its new accessories. Looking into a mirror, I still did not see myself, but a stranger, a young man looking back at me with wide blue eyes smudged underneath with dark circles, searching, searching.

The day of my release, Cindy entered the room with the usual tray and chipmunk-patterned yellow scrubs. She set the tray in my lap and moved to the curtains.

"Big day," she chirped, as light from the brightening day spilled across my bedsheets.

"Big day," I agreed, biting into a piece of toast. I chewed slowly, deliberately. My mouth hurt constantly, because I still kept biting my own tongue. It was like trying to get used to talking and eating around a live snake. I was still growing accustomed to the idea that my tongue was a part of my own body that I could control.

Cindy sat down on the chair beside my bed.

"How are you feeling . . . Alek?"

She had spoken my name for the first time. I paused, doing an internal check, my mind focusing on various parts of my body. I could feel some of the blank places, the organs that I knew were functioning, but couldn't consciously sense. I was still growing accustomed to that feeling of not knowing exactly what was going on in my body. When I was a machine, my parts were all connected, sending detailed diagnoses of performance levels. Even as my human brain grew, I was still able to hone in on my various mechanical bits. Now that I was fully human, I wasn't as attuned to all my inner workings as I had once been. Beyond the dull ache of my body's continual growing and healing from the surgeries, I could feel my heart beating against my ribs; I knew my lungs were filling with air by the expansion of my chest. I could sometimes feel food winding its way through my intestines, and I had learned by the dull grumble what hunger felt and sounded like; and it didn't take long for me to notice when I needed to empty my bladder and bowels. But I couldn't sense the blood's long journey through my heart, the arteries, the veins, and back again. I didn't know how my liver and my kidneys were doing. I needed the word of the doctor to reassure me that they were functioning. The lack of sensation was disconcerting, though, like losing one's sense of sight.

A loaded question, to ask one how one was feeling, yet most people only answer perfunctorily, a ritual greeting.

"I feel well," I told Cindy.

"You know," she looked down at her hands. "I've had a hard time knowing how to treat you."

"You're not the first," I reassured her. She smiled slightly.

"Yes, but I've struggled with what or who I'm treating. You've been nothing but a model patient, despite all the pain and learning your body has had to endure. I owe you an apology. In my mind, you were nothing but a jumble of body parts. I didn't see the whole."

"That's okay. I'm still struggling myself to feel like a whole and not just bits and pieces sewn together."

"You have a lot of people waiting for you to take you back, um, home." Cindy reddened slightly at the last word, unsure of its use. She stood up and put a hand on my shoulder.

"Good luck, Alek."

"Thanks."

Ever since being tipped off, the press had been relentless in their attempts to capture an image of me during my recovery, but heavy security provided by TARIA had prevented anyone from seeing me, beyond my usual crew of nurses, physiotherapists, and doctors who had cared for me for the past eight months. No one outside the hospital knew what I looked like or to which household I belonged. Bean's small but trustworthy group of friends had kept quiet about my transformation. Bean told me they had been asking about me, curious to see me, but of course, they had been forbidden to visit.

The hospital staff was joined by Catherine, Sebastien, and Sabine, all lining the corridor outside my room. Mick pushed me in my wheelchair down the hall and out a back door. Someone in the hospital had purposely hinted at a false release date to the media; they were expecting me tomorrow. Mick helped me into the community car that the Archambaults had rented for the big event—my return to their home. I couldn't quite call it a homecoming. I could feel a buzzing surrounding me, an excitement, an expectation. I couldn't share in the feeling; my bodily sensations overwhelmed me as I sat down heavily in the car.

"Good luck, Buddy," Mick smiled as he closed the door. Bean sat down beside me and grabbed my hand, squeezing it, until Catherine entered the vehicle and turned around, glaring at her daughter. Bean gave my hand one last squeeze, and released it. The car pulled silently from the back alleyway. Dr. Pam, Mick, Cindy, and the others all waved together.

I placed my palm on the window, removing it only once we had turned the corner and were out of sight.

15 / ACCLIMATIZATION

"There is love in me the likes of which you've never seen. There is rage in me the likes of which should never escape.

– Mary Shelley, *Frankenstein*

I TIRED QUICKLY, felt constantly achy. I needed to rest. Despite that the surgeries continued to leave me exhausted after the smallest exertion, I didn't sleep until nighttime, when the rest of the household went to bed. Catherine did nothing to hide her discomfort at my newly developing routines. She let me sleep in the basement spare room only after Dr. Pam insisted that my healing and my body's acceptance of itself depended on regular human patterns of wakefulness and sleep. I made her uncomfortable. She didn't know where to look when I stood in front of her, and ended up staring at my hands, the appendages that I had had the longest, to which she had grown the most accustomed.

At Dr. Pam's orders, I was working at half the efficiency of my regular schedule. Sebastien, Bean, and even Catherine often had to assist me by cutting up vegetables for dinner, answering incoming calls, and ignoring the things that were left undone. They often ate dinner out as I sat at the breakfast bar with a dish of reheated leftovers. I still had a difficult time with the physical process of consuming and digesting food, and felt embarrassment at the other human bodily functions that followed.

In order to hide the secret of my transformation, Bean wasn't allowed to have friends over to the house. Catherine and Sebastien didn't know that she had already shared the secret with Kate, Kimber, Russell, and Shawn. Regardless, the days were long and lonely without Bean coming home with a friend or two. Bean herself was busy at school and often didn't come home until late. I sensed an unease from Bean whenever we were left alone together, and Catherine seemed determined to make sure it rarely happened.

My memory had holes that never existed before. It sometimes took me several beats before I could recall why I was walking up the stairs at a particular moment or what I had already prepared for dinner in the past week. The time stamp had long ago faded from my consciousness and with it, the connection to Intelli!net had been severed. I retained much of the random knowledge that I learned from Intelli!net, which used to constantly run in the background when I was more mechanical than biological. My learned knowledge came up at the strangest times, firing neurons making often incomprehensible connections between situation and information.

In the past, I experienced my many emotions only in my head, but once my body was retrofitted, I understood when people said they felt things in their heart, in their stomachs. I learned the specific physical sensations that accompanied the various emotions. A lightness in my chest meant happiness; a tightening was dread. Sadness was an all-encompassing drag on my lungs. Excitement was a stirring in my gut. My brain began to make a connection with emotion and the physical sensations that accompanied them.

A definite difference exists between how humans perceive the various parts that make up their physical selves and how robots feel. SimAids sense things, but don't feel a connection to the sensations. It's simply a way of being aware of the world around us. Humans feel everything as if it is happening to them. We have a very egotistical way of perceiving the world, as if the world is inflicted upon ourselves. Most humans don't understand that we are a part of the world and the world is a part of us. We are just sensing an extension of ourselves, the same as feeling our hands or being aware of the tops of our scalps. If all humans recognized our connection to the world around us, there would be no need for an Environmental Movement; we'd already live with a natural awareness of our small but integral part in the universe.

My head was down as we ran through the rain, trying to dodge puddles. For the first time, I enjoyed being caught in a warm July downpour. As Bean and I walked past a bus shelter on our way back from a Doctor Pam-directed therapeutic walk, my shoulder connected with someone hard and unyielding.

"Sorry about that," I said, looking up, then froze. It was Jay. He was on his phone, and hadn't seen where he was going. He was my height, but slightly wider. He pocketed his phone and swiped at the wet hair dripped into his eyes

"Watch it," he glared at me quickly, his face blank, showing no recognition. He turned his head and noticed Bean, his mouth pulling into an ugly smile.

"This your new boyfriend, Bean? He must be blind, 'cause why else would he be with you?"

Anger flooded me as I remembered our last encounter. I took a step closer.

"Do you not know me?"

Bean put a hand on my arm.

Jay stopped, irritated. "What?"

"I'm the Tin Man."

His face morphed into incomprehension, then sudden recognition.

"What the hell?"

"I owe you something," I spoke menacingly, taking a step forward. Jay stepped backwards, his heels hitting the side of the bus shelter.

"Listen buddy, it was all a joke. You know what a joke is, don't you?"

"I don't care about what you said to me, but you made Bean feel horrible."

"Alek, it's okay," Bean insisted, pulling on my arm.

"What do you want, an apology? Whatever. I—" Jay stopped talking as I raised my fist and pulled it back, right at the level of his head. We both stood motionless for several beats. I slowly lowered my arm, my fist still clenched.

"I'm more human than you'll ever be," I spoke softly.

The whirring electric hum of a bus stopping caused me to turn.

Jay brushed roughly by me and hopped on as the door opened. As the bus driver scanned Jay's Intelli!chip to pay for the ride, he kept the door open and looked at me expectantly as if he thought I was getting on. I waved him on, and began walking away, smiling, despite the aching tension in my shoulder.

"You may look normal now, but you're still a freak! You both are!" Jay shouted from the safety of the moving bus.

Bean's arm dropped as I pulled away and began walking again, hunched over. Was that how people considered me? If they didn't know any better, they'd think I was human. But once they knew the truth, was I seen as an other?

"Are you okay?" Bean ran out in front of me to stop me. She touched my arms, looked at my face, searching for pain. It was the first time since coming home from TARIA that she had really looked at me, that I had felt her touch.

"I'm okay. I wanted to hit him."

"But you didn't." She withdrew her hand.

"No. I'm worried he's going to tell someone though, alert the press to who I am."

"He's too scared of you. Did you see his face when he realized who you are? I don't think he'll say anything."

"I should have told him I was your cousin visiting from Montreal."

Bean smiled reassuringly and pulled me into a hug. We stood in the rain; I felt as though I was melting as I accepted her touch. I was a patchwork of a person, not quite complete, and still, she pulled me to her, touching my human-ness. Gratitude for Bean and her ability to see me whole flooded through me. I wrapped my arms around her and returned the embrace. I was keenly aware of every inch of her body that touched mine. Neurons fired down newly-created paths, overwhelming my consciousness with sensation. I let go and stood back, feeling dizzy.

As we continued walking, I started to feel dozens of pairs of eyes on . . . me. I began noticing a few sideways glances, some second takes, and outright stares. Was I imagining it all?

"Geez Bean, what did you do? You made me choose an awful face."

"What are you talking about?"

"Can't you see?" I spoke in a low tone, "People are looking at me."

"Yes," Bean's eyes crinkled at me. I crossed my arms around my body, feeling uncomfortably self-conscious.

"Why are they staring? How can they tell I was a SimAid?" I said, confused.

"No," she said impatiently. "Look." She stopped and turned me to face the darkened window of a store for lease. "What do you see?"

I couldn't see much in the store. Some boxes, piles of dead flies on the windowsill. Then I realized what she was looking at. Us. Our image reflected on the window like two ghosts looking out onto the bright world. Bean, with her heart-shaped face, wide eyes and mouth always twitching in a smile. Me, with . . . my face. My eyes. My nose. My mouth. It was all so . . . symmetrical. Yet, it was me. My brain had finally made the connection and had recognized that face as belonging to me.

I saw us.

"What's wrong with how I look?" I asked. As I peered into the storefront, I could see myself staring intently. I looked nothing like the composite picture that had been created in Dr. Pam's office. There was something different behind my eyes. I couldn't explain it.

"Why don't I look like the photo?" I wasn't sure if this was good or bad, just different.

"You look like I'd expect you to look with a face that expresses your insides." Bean stared at me much the same way I peered in the window at my pale reflection. "It's the specific way you wear that face," she continued. "Pure curiosity. No self-consciousness." I raised my eyebrows slightly.

She pointed at my face. "That's it! It's that constant quizzical, interested expression, as if you're trying to figure out the whole world."

I continued to look at our ghostlike reflections, trying to see the face that Bean saw.

"You're very handsome," she added, smiling up at me. Without meaning to, I felt my face reflect a similar expression.

Later that evening, back at the house, I stood at the mirror, examining my face. Reaching up a hand, I tentatively touched my cheek. It was soft, giving way slightly, yet I could feel the hardness of the bone beneath. I smiled, or at least tried, but only achieved the effect of stretching my lips wide and baring my teeth in a grimace. How to smile? I thought of Bean and her quick bursts of laughter like a shower of sparkling stones. In the mirror I saw my face form a real smile at the thought of Bean. My lips stretched luxuriously and something in my eyes changed. They brightened, crinkled a bit at the outer edges. Bean, I thought again, and my smile deepened. The muscles in my face pulled back and I looked . . . like me. This was how I felt. Happy.

16 / ADRENALINE

"SIT," BEAN COMMANDED. We were outside in the back-yard by the tire swing. It was an unusually cool and blustery day for the end of summer. Bean had decided it was time that I tried swinging. She showed me how to hook my legs through the hole in the middle of the tire. I didn't fit as easily as she did, but I scrunched up, my legs sticking straight out on one side, the rest of my body straining to hold on tightly to the other side.

"Now what?"

"Now hold on while I push you," she said as she pulled the tire back as far as she could go. I felt gravity tugging against her efforts, against the tire, against me. When Bean let go, I sucked in a breath as I swung in a small arc under the tree. The wind cooled my face and shushed across my ears. Bean pushed on the tire, this time using the gathering speed to slingshot me higher.

The air whooshed around me, and my body felt strange as the pull down towards the earth loosened briefly when I slowed at the top of the arc. I felt like I was flying! But I couldn't really control it. The sensation had a rhythm of its own with each rise and fall of the swing.

And then I knew what Bean meant about swinging and the feeling of being alive. I was firmly attached to the reality of this earth, but at the same time, I felt like I could be anyone or do anything . . . I felt that I could fly.

Bean stopped pushing when I got the rhythm of pumping my legs to keep the swing going on my own. I still tired easily, however, and my new muscles weren't as toned as they should have been, so she began pushing me again once my body gave out.

"Remember when you first came to us? You asked me on the swing about why I was an only child."

"You said that your parents never meant to have you," I said.

"It feels weird knowing you're an accident." Bean spoke matter-of-factly.

"I'm an accident too, don't forget. I wasn't supposed to want to be more than I was."

"You've always been different," Bean insisted. "I don't know how or why, but you were never like the rest of your kind. Not since the beginning."

She never called me a robot. I found it sweetly endearing that Bean always saw me as potential, as something other, as me, never a servant or a machine.

"Hey," Bean spoke abruptly, with a hand in the pocket of her jeans. She pulled out a long rectangular package. "You've never had the chance to try chocolate yet, have you?"

"What? No." I'd been continuing to follow Dr. Pam's strict diet, trying to ease my digestive system into various foods.

"Here." Bean broke off a dark brown square and handed it to me. I sniffed it curiously; it reminded me of freshly turned spring earth and brewed coffee. I stuck my tongue out and touched the tip to the square. Hm. Nothing much.

"No, put it in your mouth."

I stuck the square in my mouth and waited as it warmed. A bean-y brown flavour, with bitter bite and a mellow sweet, creamy taste flooded my taste buds: Chocolate.

"Good, huh?" Bean grinned at the look of surprise and delight on my face. I never thought that the sense of taste could bring so much pleasure.

"Now I understand why the Aztecs and Mayans used cacao beans as currency. This is amazing."

"Residual random Intelli!net knowledge?" Bean asked, grinning.

I nodded, chewing thoughtfully on the remaining piece. I began to swing again with my head tilted back, feeling the wind tousling my hair, watching the clouds scuttle across the grey sky above me, hearing the rhythmic creak of the swing rope grating on the tree branch, smelling the musty, wormy air of a recent downpour, tasting the remnants of chocolate on my tongue.

"You know, the world is much more interesting with all five functioning senses."

"If you're only using five, you're missing one," Bean said, giving me an extra hard push.

"What are you talking about? I have a sense of smell, of taste, of touch, of sight, of hearing. That's all five senses."

"You're missing the sixth." I could tell by the slight pull at the corners of her mouth that she was joking.

"Even you aren't clairvoyant," I said.

"I'm not talking about ESP, I'm talking about the other sixth sense." Her smirk widened into a near-smile.

"What's that?"

"Your sense of humour."

"Oh."

"Ha, ha!" Bean spoke the words instead of laughing. "It's a joke, silly!"

"If that was a joke, then you seem to be deficient in the sixth sense as well." I grinned and hopped off the swing, wincing slightly at the jolt of pain in my joints as I landed. "Ugh. Not quite whole yet," I said, rubbing my knees.

"Whole enough," Bean replied. "You're more Alek than ever before."

Smiling, she took my hands and held them for a moment. Warmth flooded my fingertips and palms, spreading up my arms and into my chest. Inexplicably, my heart began pounding at her touch. Bean looked at my face, then quickly down at our hands.

"Ooh, your hand are freezing! Let's go in. It's getting too cold out." She let go and ran towards the house.

We walked through the back door into the breezeway. Bean flung her coat over a hook and rushed into the warm kitchen. As I placed my hand-me-down coat from Sebastien over the hook, I noticed something on the floor below Bean's hastily placed coat; presumably it had fallen from a pocket. I leaned down and saw that it was a small notebook with a scratched cover and dog-eared pages. I had seen this book before in Bean's room. I picked it up and opened it, recognizing immediately the handwriting in Bean's journal. I knew I shouldn't read it, but I couldn't resist:

It's very odd to see him move now. He walks as though his body is something extra he's carrying around with him. His arms don't swing with the opposing leg as he walks, but hang at his sides, with palms as open as his face. His legs move gracefully, yet in a sort of mechanical way.

Bean. This was her journal. And this description must be me. Did I really want to find out how Bean saw me? This freak, this mutant consciousness in a lab-made body? Shame filled my gut and I quickly dropped the journal. I struggled with conflicting emotions until curiosity won over, and I found my unwilling hand reach again for the notebook.

But he's exactly what I dreamed the real Alek would look like: Thick black hair, his bi-coloured eyes with enlarged pupils like the dots on a pair of question marks; his eyebrows nearly furrowing in the squiggle above. His straight aquiline nose, flaring nostrils that reveal almost as much about his temperament as his eyes do. Wide, full-lipped mouth slightly darker than the average male set of lips, and pale unblemished skin. Strong, but not too jutting, jaw and cheekbones. Basically the skin of a baby on a young man. He is beautifully and strangely flawless. The kind of perfection that makes people take another look. The kind of face that makes babies automatically smile and the elderly trust him and women, well, swoon. It's hard to miss a face like that. His face, plain and open, yet so perfect. He cannot hide a single change in his thoughts or feelings. His face is as wide and open as a prairie sky, with the sudden revelation of his thoughts or feelings flitting across like changes in the weather...

I felt my cheeks grow hot; for anyone present, my embarrassment would have been plain on my face.

He is as honest as the expression in his eyes and at the corners of his mouth. He stares as if he's trying to take in the entire world, as if to remember every last detail, each gesture, every word of a conversation. How can I help but fall in love with him?

I stopped reading, nearly dropping the book. My heart pounded against the fragile walls of my chest.

How could this be? Bean, the girl who named me after a teddy bear or stray dog or pet goldfish—she loved me?

I walked around in a fog for the next few days, avoiding Bean, not sure whether I should tell her I found the journal, not sure if I should tell her . . . what? That I had growing feelings for her as well? That I was a robot-turned-human exhibiting normal human emotions towards a beautiful girl-turned-young-woman? Did I dare believe her secret confession that she had not yet shared with me?

The knowledge of Bean's feelings for me clouded my consciousness, occupied my every waking thought and even my dreams:

I am pushing Bean on the swing. She is laughing as the wind whips her hair back and forth. The sky is blue and limitless. I stop her swinging and Bean stops laughing. Her face is flushed. I am holding on to the chains just above her hands. I slip my hands on top of hers. She is still smiling as she leans towards me. Her eyes close and her face is all I can see: her long lashes, a splash of freckles across her nose, and her full lips, slightly parted, coming closer to me. I close my eyes.

I groggily became aware that I was sitting up in bed. I shook my head, not sure how I had gotten there. It dawned on me that I had been in bed the whole time, sleeping. This was a dream. Wow, a dream! So that was what they were like. Already the details slipped away from the corners of my mind. How strange! How delightful! I revelled in the sensation of Bean's lips on mine, my heart thumping in my chest as if trying to escape. I wanted to go back to sleep and continue the story. I lay down again and closed my eyes, willing myself to sleep. I just managed to achieve fuller alertness.

That morning, Bean left for school before I had a chance to see her. I had been sleeping later, still recovering from the incredible energy it took for my body to heal and grow. Luckily, Dr. Pam had made it quite clear to the Archambault family that I could not be expected to resume normal tasks at least for a few months.

17 / ANGUISH

"Man," I cried, "how ignorant art thou in thy pride of wisdom!
– Mary Shelley, *Frankenstein*

IT WAS LATE afternoon, and I was supposed to be cleaning the silverware in the dining room, but I could hear Catherine and Sebastien's urgent whispers wafting through the crack in the French doors leading to the living room.

"This is going too far. He's not quite sane, I think," said the lower voice insistently, it was Sebastien.

"Don't you see? We're on the cusp of redefining humanity. This could mean the difference between TARIA being a world leading Robotics company and THE only robotics company worldwide. We will be names in science textbooks for centuries! We're talking about immortality!"

"And Sabine? How is this going to affect her?"

"It's about time that our daughter gave up childish games and finally grew up. She's played with her little imaginary playmate for far too long now. If she hasn't decided she's quite ready to leave playing with toys in her childhood, then we'll just have to make that decision for her. She's nearly eighteen years old for God's sake! She should be thinking about her future. Does she really think that playing a cello is some kind of career?"

"What do you mean?" Bean had come into the house quietly. Her hair spilled out from under a wool hat, and she held her cello case close to her side. Catherine looked momentarily alarmed, but regained her composure quickly. Sebastien moved towards his daughter.

"Honey, what your mother means is—"

"What I mean is when you picked up that infernal instrument at eight years old, we thought it was a quirky phase. Your little hobby charmed our friends at parties, gave you something to do by yourself, since you seemed to shun all other children your age. But we didn't think it would last!"

Bean shook her hair out from under her hat and placed her cello case down.

"But it did last, didn't it? And it's so disappointing to you that I don't follow in your footsteps, pursuing a career in the glorious field of science and technology. Well, guess what? I love music, and I love the cello. I will never stop playing! In fact, I applied to a College of Music in Montreal and was accepted. I've already looked into housing and there are tons of affordable apartments available."

"And how are you going to pay for this schooling and these living arrangements?"

"I'll get a job. I'll wait tables, busk in the subway, whatever it takes."

I could tell that the busking comment really got under Catherine's skin. I was sure she couldn't bear the thought of a child of hers begging on the streets.

"Montreal is a big, dangerous city. You're so young and naive."

"First I'm too old to keep playing the cello, but I'm too young to work in a big city by myself? Make up your mind, Mother. Am I too old or too young?"

"Maybe we should all just take a breath. Let's sit down. Talk it out rationally." Sebastien stood now between his wife and daughter, looking at both of them, his eyes pleading for them to stop. I pitied him, this man caught in the middle. He obviously loved both of them and saw both points of view.

Bean wiped her eyes. "I'm done talking. It's done. I've been accepted. I'm legally of age to leave this house and your control."

"Honey, we don't want you to disappear from our lives." Sebastien touched his daughter's arm. He tried to hug her, but she backed away.

"I want to ask Alek to come with me too. He needs a fresh start."

Catherine blinked and abruptly turned to me, as if she was surprised to see me through the glass in the French doors.

"Go to the charging closet," she commanded.

"But—" I wanted to remind her that I no longer needed charging.

"Are you arguing with me?" she spluttered. "You can't argue! You're not a person! I . . . I bought you!"

"That justification has been used for centuries to subjugate those who are different, to deny their humanity," I said quietly.

"Go!" she screamed, her face contorted in a mask more

inhuman than any cybernetic creation.

I quietly walked into the closet, feeling extremely ridiculous. I left the doors open, so I could see and hear the conversation. Out of habit, it seemed that the moment I was in the charging closet, Catherine ceased to acknowledge that I could see and hear everything.

"What do you mean?" She now spoke so quietly that I had to strain to hear her voice. Bean looked at her mother with pity.

"You can't possibly think he's going to continue to live with you now that he's human. He's not your property any longer. Slavery was abolished a long time ago, Mother. Alek needs to start his life in a place where no one knows about his unconventional beginnings." There was a pleading note to Bean's words.

"His unconventional . . . " Catherine paused, and a little sigh escaped from her lips. "My darling. He still belongs to us. No one has granted his freedom. He's a unique case. He is part of a larger plan. He always has been." Sebastien shot her a warning look, but she continued to speak.

"You wonder why this whole experimentation has been allowed to continue, to be funded. The SimAid is part of an even bigger plan than you can imagine. Trent is going to use Alek."

I felt a sudden chill across my body as if a cold draft had swept by me. My new-found freedom was all a lie?

"Mother, what on earth are you talking about?"

Catherine sighed as she sat down on the couch. She reached for her daughter's hand, but Bean pulled away.

"I tried to protect you, not let you get too close. Alek's brain, Alek's body will soon be Trent's."

Bean's whole body stopped as if someone had flipped a switch and turned her off.

"Wha . . . what?"

"Adam Trent is going to attempt a revolutionary procedure. He's allowed the development of Alek's brain, because he wants it pristine, unmarred, ready to take in the sum of Trent's consciousness. That's why Trent used his own brain cells—he wanted to ease the uploading of his consciousness. Trent wants to move into Alek's body eventually. That was his intention the whole time, even before he became ill. We've been planning it ever since he told me about Alek's biological brain. Adam is going to upload his consciousness into the developed brain—he will take over the body that we've grown. The SimAid has never been anything but a shell—a body reserved for someone else."

I was never meant to be human, but a house for someone else's consciousness. In the darkness, I looked down at the dim outline of my hands, these hands that were never my own. I felt a disconnect from my body as I sagged against the closet doorframe.

"But he's not someone else! You can't even say his name! He's Alek!" Bean's stiff body was shaking now.

"He's a freak—not even of nature—but by design. He's Frankenstein's monster. Do you think our goal was to create a human from a robot? What purpose would that serve? We have enough defective humanity walking around this world already! Don't you see? He's the key to immortal consciousness! He is a new body ready to be slipped into."

"He's not an article of clothing—a pair of gloves!" Bean's voice matched her mother's frequency and volume.

"Of course that's all he is!" Catherine snapped. "And it's about time you've come to terms with that."

"You're wrong! He's the only true friend I've ever had! He's always accepted me, and I've accepted him." Bean took a breath, then said quietly but with conviction, "I love him."

Catherine stood as still as a recharging SimAid. Her face slowly turned from pink to red.

"You love him!?" she hissed.

Bean's admission came bursting out, like a geyser exploding from deep within her. "I do," Bean sobbed. "I am in love with Alek."

"He's not even human! It's disgusting! You're in love with a . . . a, family computer! A program . . . " her mother sputtered. She wrung her long fingers together and paced the room as if trying to escape this appalling reality but not sure quite how or where to go.

I stood by the door as quietly as if I were in sleep mode. Strange feelings flittered through me. Bean loved me. She did! I felt like running and shouting through the entire house. Another part of me whispered the frightful thought: I could be terminated. I was shaken to the very core. I didn't want to leave this world. I wouldn't leave Bean! But how? I had no rights; I wasn't even a person in the eyes of the law.

"You will go to Montreal. With my blessing! You will immerse yourself fully in this music program you're so passionate about, and you will go without Alek! You may be able to leave this house legally, but it—" She stressed the pronoun, pointing a long, trembling finger towards me in the closet, "—belongs to us! This is unhealthy! You need distance to see this situation rationally."

Bean ran from the room and out into the hall, past my closet and up the stairs to her bedroom. I felt the house shake as she slammed the door. I strained to hear her, but nothing. Not a sob or a muffled scream. Silence. I heard footsteps as Catherine walked quickly towards the hallway. I thought for a moment that she was going to go after her daughter, go apologize, tell her she was sorry, but she stopped at my charging closet.

"For your own good—and hers," she whispered into the crack of the door before shutting it firmly. I heard the click of the lock on the handle that had never been used before. I reached out a hand and grasped the handle from the inside, hoping that I was wrong, that the door might open. It didn't.

Several hours went by. My legs ached and shook. I barely had enough room to stand, let alone sit down. I took to leaning against the back of the closet. My mind drifted far from the darkness, trying to process what Catherine had said: My body was Trent's. He was going to upload his consciousness into my mind. What would happen to my consciousness? What would happen to me?

What would happen to Bean?

Finally I heard Catherine walk quietly to the door and unlock it. She turned her body away before speaking to me.

"Dinner."

So this is how it would be. I was only to come out when needed like a broom used only for sweeping.

I could run away, but what about Bean? I couldn't leave her. I'm sure my face would be plastered over every Intelli!screen in the world. I'd have to go into hiding forever. People disappeared all the time; they changed their identities. No, I decided. I had to stay and fight. But first, I needed answers.

I waited until the house was dark and quiet until I snuck into the kitchen and touched the Intelli!screen to wake it from sleep mode. I scrolled down the address list until I found who I was looking for. I swiped the dial button and waited.

The screen was filled with Adam Trent's face, his skin tinged yellow. He was in the middle of wiping his mouth with a tissue. His dull eyes brightened slightly when he saw me.

"Ah, Alek. You are looking so healthy. How are you feeling?" He spoke slowly, trying to catch his breath.

"Dr. Pam says my body gets stronger every day. I still get exhausted easily."

"To be expected. What can I do for you at this late hour?" He began coughing, and I waited for him to finish.

"Why do I exist? Why have you made me human?"

Trent sighed. He spoke slowly as if weighing each word. "I wasn't expecting to speak to you directly about this. However . . ." He shrugged.

"At first, I was surprised that you wanted a human body to go along your brain. But then I realized how delightful it would be to live again in a strong, fully human body. Cybernetics are only accepted to a degree in this society. You can't have too many factory-made parts or people don't consider you to be real anymore. But I guess you know that firsthand." He grinned wolfishly and took a few struggling breaths before continuing.

"Oh, I don't intend to keep that particular body. I'll get upgrades over time to become more impervious, less biological." I waited a full minute while he coughed again. My insides felt tight.

"I missed so much of my own life, Alek, being holed up in my lab for years. I can finally have the life I never had the chance to live!"

"You had your chance at life, Trent. Now let me have mine."

"But it's not yours, Alek. You're nothing but Pinocchio wanting to be a real boy. I created you. I animated you with my own essence."

"I may have started out with your brain cells," I spit out the words, "but I am no more you than if I'd borrowed the cells from your big toe."

"I needed to ensure that you had a will to live. How would you have survived those countless surgeries had you known that I would harvest your body for my own consciousness?"

"And you tell me the truth now, why?"

"You deserve to know your destiny."

I felt my stomach clench. I slammed my hand against the screen, ending the connection, then turned sideways and vomited for the first time ever.

18 / ABSENCE

*Tin Man: Now I know I've got a heart because
it is breaking.*

– L. Frank Baum, *The Wonderful Wizard Oz*

FEELING WITHOUT THE sensation. I was numb with shock, with revelation. Bean loved me. I loved Bean. She was gone. I had no individual rights. I wasn't even human under any known laws on this planet. I was a hideous experiment that walked and talked and looked and felt real. I was a hermit crab's borrowed shell. That was all.

The enormity of my gains in the past years, and now my loss, overwhelmed me. I could do nothing but continue my duties in the Archambault house. Somewhere in my brain was the memory of what it was like to be a machine. I eased back into the mindless grind of obedient servitude. I lived the next weeks with all of my humanity pushed into a tight ball, curled up somewhere inside me.

Bean had been packed and shuffled off to Montreal somehow

without my knowledge. I was sent on errands, to the market, to the TARIA building, and in that time, Bean had disappeared. How could she have left so willingly, I wondered, so easily?

How could she have left me?

I walked around the house for the next several weeks like, well, a robot. I performed my required duties: I answered the door and phone politely, cleaned the house, made meals, and purchased groceries, the whole time thinking of Bean and what she was doing. What else could I do but the menial chores for which I was designed? I was at a loss without her.

My brain was a jumble of thoughts that I couldn't sort out. Was this the essence of humanity: indecision and uncertainty mixed with a whole array of emotions? I felt overcome: I understood the word. My thoughts had come over me and taken control.

I needed to find Bean, but how? I had no money, no identification. I wasn't even legally a person.

One morning, after Sebastien and Catherine had left for work, I began reviewing my list of chores on the Intelli!screen. Everything looked usual: empty the Intelli!vac, wash the windows, polish the silverware, pack up Sabine's room.

Pack up Bean's room.

I stopped cold. Were they trying to torture me? No, for that would mean they had a sense of my feelings for their daughter. I came to the conclusion that Catherine had no idea who I really was, of how fully their experiment had succeeded.

I walked up the stairs, my feet feeling like weights at the ends of my legs.

I stood for a long time outside her bedroom door.

I opened the door a crack. I took a breath. My lungs, still new, inflated painfully. I pushed the door wide open and stepped inside.

Bean's room looked the same as it always did. Organized chaos, she had called it. The only things missing were cello, music stand, and Bean herself.

I walked over to her closet and opened it up. Clothes had been hastily pulled off hangers, a small pile of shoes that used to lie on the floor was gone. I pulled open a few drawers in the dresser by her bed. They held very little—the odd pair of mismatched socks, a sweater. I sat on the floor, my back sliding down the side of the dresser. She was gone. I stared at the handmade sign hanging above her bed:

Music is love in search of a word.
- Sidonie

I pulled myself onto the comforter and lay facedown on her pillow. As I breathed, I could smell the soft, sweet scent of her hair from where her head used to lie. I curled up in a ball and slid my hands under the pillow. My hands had been the beginning. I cursed my hands, cursed humanity. My eyes began to prickle painfully, and I felt a wetness at the edges. Warm tears welled up in my eyes. I was crying for the first time, and I didn't care. All I cared about was the loss that flooded my entire being. I was wholly human, wholly broken. As I cried, my hands clenched something under the pillow. It felt like a book. I stopped crying and pulled it out. My heart tightened as I recognized the cover. Bean's journal. I opened the book, needing to feel close to her again. The pages fluttered open automatically to a dog-eared page. I read the familiar writing:

This is Bean's writing.
This is Alek's writing
Bean
Alek
Bean and Alek
Alek and Bean

Tears again blurred my vision. I rifled to the end of the pages. I stopped as I saw my name in bold lettering at the top of the last page. I read:

ALEK

You have always been a real person to me. You were always someone I could talk to without judgement. You saw me. And I see you for who you are. I would never willingly leave you, but there was no way to bring you with me.
You need to get away and come find me. I need you.

I love you.

There was an address on the bottom of the letter, I guessed for her school or an apartment.

Something awoke inside me, the human part of me that had been hidden swelled and filled my entire body with light. I had a purpose; but how could I get away? Sebastien and Catherine would be home in mere hours. It wasn't enough time for me to make my escape. I'd need to leave early in the morning to give me time.

I ran downstairs and accessed the family schedule. The Archambaults were attending a conference in Toronto later in the week. It was a packed, three day schedule. Perfect. This would be the longest, most torturous wait ever, but I would do it. Before I made my escape, I had someone to visit one last time.

I didn't know where Adam Trent lived. For all I knew, he didn't even have a home. I had only ever seen him at the Archambault's and at work. I was nervous about going to TARIA to seek him out, but I didn't have a choice.

As I walked through the large glass doors, my heart pounded furiously. I glanced quickly up at the TARIA logo: a human hand reaching towards a robotic one, fingers almost touching, intentionally reminiscent of Michaelangelo's painting on the ceiling of the Sistine Chapel, of God's hand reaching out towards Adam's. I smiled bitterly at such self-importance.

I hurried through the lobby, trying to appear purposeful, as though I knew where I was going. What if someone recognized me? What if I ran into Catherine or Sebastien? As I approached the information desk, I attempted to look inconspicuous, as if I belonged.

"Can I help you?" It was the same receptionist who had stopped Bean and I the last time we had been here. Now I was just a chaperone without a girl to watch over.

"I'm visiting Adam Trent on the . . . " I sifted through my memories quickly, "fourth floor."

The receptionist stared at me. This is it, I thought, she knows who I am. She knows I've run away. Any moment now she'll call down the Archambaults to come pick up their SimAid.

"Who are you?" she asked, her hand hovering over the Intelli!screen. I shifted my weight from one foot to the other. Trying to remain calm, to look confident.

"I'm his, uh, nephew." She stared at me a moment longer. Her eyes softened. "Have you come from far away?"

"Um, yes?" I couldn't understand why she was asking me these questions.

"You must not know. He's been hospitalized, dear. He hasn't been to work in weeks."

"In weeks." I repeated dumbly. Yes, I knew Trent had been ill, but so ill that he'd not even been to his lab?

"He's in the TARIA medical building, of course. We take care of our own. The building's across the road. Here's the room number." She scribbled something down on a slip of paper.

"Thank you," I said, stunned and relieved. "That's very kind."

Minutes later, I stood in the main corridor of the medical building with coloured lines on the floor showing the way to various departments. Luckily, I didn't run into anyone familiar. During my transformation, I had stayed in a remote wing of the building where only specific employees were granted security access.

I walked along a golden strip of paint to oncology. I couldn't help it – I started humming "Follow the Yellow Brick Road" from The Wizard of Oz. I giggled inappropriately. A man shuffling with an IV stopped and stared at me, probably wondering if I had lost my way from the mental health floor.

I sobered as I slowed down outside the room. From beyond the open door, I heard nothing except for the small symphony of rhythmic pings and shushings of various machines. Taking a deep breath, I walked in. Adam lay face up staring at the ceiling. His chest rose and fell with obvious difficulty. Tubes ran from his arms and into his nose. Multicoloured wires snaked their way across his chest and under the blankets.

I thought about my time with my new heart, new lungs; the pain it caused. Mine had been a pain of newness, of breaking in. His was a pain of breaking down, of cessation.

"Adam." He turned his head slowly, almost mechanically to look at me. His lip trembled as his eyes took in my new form. He looked infinitely old, as though he had always lain there in that hospital bed.

"Alek?" He spoke with great effort, taking a shallow breath after the word. His face was rigid, unmoving.

"It's me. All me," I said. I took his hand, not out of empathy, but to let him feel my warm, living skin. He squeezed my hand tentatively and turned it slowly in his own pale, withered one. For one brief moment, I considered taking my hands and placing them on his neck, squeezing until the life dribbled out of him; but then I would never be free. I'd be an experiment gone horribly wrong.

"The irony . . . is not lost on . . . me," he spoke laboriously, his hands tugged weakly at the tube lying across his chest. Sitting down on a chair by the bed, I leaned over him and looked into his eyes.

"I wanted to ask you . . . to tell you . . . I'm leaving. I want to live."

"So do I. Does that make me evil?" A machine wheezed in time to his breaths.

"No," I stepped back from the bed. "It's just instinct."

"And you know so much about instinct now," Trent's smile looked more like the grimace of a skeleton.

"I know all about instinct and human desire to be more than our needs."

"What, then?"

"Our wishes, our dreams. My desire to be human."

"You were always meant to be more than the sum of your parts," he spoke as his hand moved to a button by the bed. He pressed on it weakly, sighing, then began to cough, his whole body shaking in the effort.

Out of the corner of my eye, I saw two large men dressed as orderlies looming in the doorway. As they took a step towards me, I backed into Trent's hospital bed. I felt a firm grip on my arm as Trent held me with sudden strength.

"This is for the good of humanity, Alek." A shadow loomed, and I felt a pinch in the back of my head.

Then oblivion.

I awakened groggily, slowly becoming aware that I was lying down. I felt pressure at my wrists and ankles. I attempted to move, then realized that I was strapped in. I turned my head, noting the white walls, slow drip of an IV into my arm, a dark Intelli!screen on the wall. I could hear voices outside in the hall.

A nurse walked in, then stopped quickly upon seeing my

eyes open.

"Oh. You're awake. I just . . . " she faltered, unsure of what to tell me.

"Why am I here?" No answer. She busied herself with changing the IV bag, then hurried out again.

What could I do? Escape was impossible. Appealing to her humanity felt like a cruel joke. She obviously saw me exactly the way Trent did.

Just then, Dr. Pam walked into the room, no doubt summoned by the nurse.

"Dr. Pam! Where is Adam Trent? Why can't I leave?"

Dr. Pam looked down at me, tears making her eyes sparkle.

"I'm sorry, Alek. It's the law. There's no precedent for this procedure. They technically still own you."

"But what can I do?" I whispered, defeated. She took my hand.

"Alek, I had no idea what I was getting myself into when I agreed to head your transformational surgeries. I didn't realize I was dealing with a living being. I am truly sorry. I can only promise you that I'll make sure this never happens again." The tears sparkling in her eyes spilled over, slipping down her cheeks.

"But where's Trent?"

"He's being prepped for surgery. I'm sorry. It's out of my hands." She squeezed my arm, then hurried out the door.

A surge of panic hit me, as a wave of adrenalin coursed through my young body, my survival instincts overwhelming me. I strained against the restraints, shouting hoarsely. Another nurse came in. She replaced the bag of my IV. As the medicine dripped into my arm, I became drowsy and fought to stay awake. I fought . . . I fight . . . I lose . .

Blurred shapes, dark movements, indistinct voices.

I feel pain, which makes me feel relieved that I still feel anything at all, then no pain.

A scream. Was it mine?

A voice I know, saying my name over and over. Alek. Alek. Alek.

Come back to me.

19 / ACTION

Life, although it may only be an accumulation of anguish, is dear to me, and I will defend it.
– Mary Shelley, *Frankenstein*

I FELT AS though seconds had passed over the course of years. My throat felt dry and sore. I gagged. Somebody spoke, "Just breathe out, I'll remove it."

I breathed and choked as a length of what felt like barbed wire was removed from my esophagus. I attempted to open my eyes. Dr. Pam stood over me.

I am still me, I realized as I tried to look down to see if my body was still there. I couldn't move my head enough, so instead I attempted to send a signal from my brain to my hand, hoping that they were both still attached. Slowly, I felt the recognition of a part of my own body moving above the sheet. I directed it into my line of sight—my hand! It trembled in front of my eyes, whole, attached. With difficulty, I shifted my gaze to Dr. Pam, who was smiling.

"You're awake."

"I'm not . . . him?"

"No. You're Alek." Her smile turned down somewhat at the corners. Her eyes looked sad.

"What happened?"

"Trent didn't have much time left. Catherine and Sebastien had called to warn him that you might try to find him. He was waiting for you with a team of doctors on call to do his bidding. He had you prepped and ready for the consciousness transfer. What he didn't expect was that he would not survive the procedure."

"How?"

Dr. Pam rubbed her eyes tiredly. "He had cancer. It snuck up on him in the last few months and took over most of his body. I imagine he was too focused on you and your progress to pay attention to the warning signs of his own body. He died even before they attempted the uploading."

She sighed and sat down on the chair beside the bed.

"As scientists, we sometimes feel that we are gods, until we encounter the one barrier we can't remove. We've eradicated many diseases, but not all of them. There will always be a new illness to replace a strain we've conquered."

"And me?"

"Nothing's changed. You belong to the Archambault family." Her eyes brimmed with tears. "Alek, I'm sorry."

"For what? Sorry that you made me human? For your own human failings?"

"I'm sorry for all the pain it's caused you."

"What's humanity without the pain?" I said simply. I didn't

know anymore what humanity was. I took the pain with everything else. Now one thought occupied my brain.

"Where's Bean? Does she know?"

"She's been here. From what I've heard, her mother sent her
back to Montreal. Like it or not, I'm involved. But I've chosen
sides now, Alek. I will fight for you. I will gladly stand up and
defend your rights as an individual in court. For now, hopefully
this makes up for my responsibility in this . . . experiment," she
spoke the last word as if it left an unpleasant taste. "Sabine left
this for you."

Dr. Pam took a small piece of folded paper out of her pocket
and put it in my hand. She then turned and walked out the door
without looking back at me.

My hands, still weak and trembling, unfolded the paper. On
it was written the same Montreal address, only with an added
date and time for an evening three days from now. Bean mustn't
have been sure that I got her first message.

How was I going to make it?

I pulled the tubes and sensors from various parts of my body
and wrenched myself upright, heaving myself from the bed. I
stumbled down the corridors in my paper gown, gripping the
walls. My body felt sluggish because of my former state of seda-
tion and my legs were slow and clumsy in obeying the signals
my brain was sending. I guessed from the muted lighting and the
near silence of the hall that it was night. As I lurched forward,
I heard voices coming from around the corner. It was Sebastien
and Catherine.

"This is wrong. Everything about this whole experiment
from the beginning. I kept my mouth shut, Catherine, but I

can't any longer."

"Well, Sebastien, you have nothing to worry about since Trent's dead. Alek is safe."

"But is he free?" They had stopped in the adjoining hallway.

"What on earth do you mean?" Catherine's anger was mingled with confusion. "He belongs to us. TARIA can't even touch him now. With Trent dead, Alek is my intellectual property."

"He's not intellectual property anymore. The procedures may belong to you and Trent, but Alek is human now. He's a person!"

"You were always too soft for this line of work, Sebastien. You let your emotions get in the way of progress."

"Not emotions, ethics. And remember, Cat, you fell in love with me for being soft. You always said that I saved you from a loveless life."

"I see now that youth is perpetually tinged with melodrama. Sabine's youth, our youth." Catherine's hard tone gave way to regret. I heard footfalls.

Quickly, I pushed against the nearest door and practically fell into the room, hoping it was empty. Turning to scan the room, I noticed a figure lying on the bed, a sheet draped over the face. A covered face could only mean one thing. I padded over to the body and carefully pulled the sheet down. Trent's pale and still figure appeared. Death had erased the worried lines above his eyes. Waves of varying emotions swept through me, threatening to knock me over, as I stood over this man who had wanted to take my life for his own. I examined the thin arm and slender hand that poked out of the sheet.

"You owe me," I whispered.

I looked around the room, realizing that someone would be

back at any moment for the body. I spotted a tray sitting on a rolling cart that must have been abandoned in the moments before Trent's death. I found what I was looking for, picked it up, and walked back over to the body.

Trent's eyes were closed but somehow, I felt as though he was watching me.

I gently grasped his hand and pulled it closer to me. His skin was pale and cool, but not yet unyielding. I took the scalpel in my hand and sliced into his arm. A rivulet of blood wound sluggishly down the arm and dripped onto the floor as I dug around under his skin, searching. Finally, I felt a hard small strip of metal. With my fingers, I pulled back the flap of skin and carefully removed the Intelli!chip from Trent's arm. I took a clean towel and wiped the blood from the floor and wrapped his arm, tucking it back under the sheet.

The door opened.

I whirled around, my guilt obvious by the bloody scalpel in my hand; I closed my fist quickly over the Intelli!chip. Sebastien stood in the doorway, taking in the situation, then closed the door behind him. Catherine was nowhere to be seen. He spoke slowly.

"Alek, I'm not going to hurt you."

"I don't wish you any harm either, Sebastien, but I need to find Bean."

"I understand," he continued to speak calmly while standing still, as if approaching a wild animal. Sebastien obviously felt I would do anything to get away; I realized that he was right.

"You can't use Adam Trent's chip, though, Alek; they'll know it's been stolen, and they'll deactivate it."

What was I thinking? That I would simply take his chip and take over his life the way he had tried to take mine? How foolishly I had acted.

"I want to help you Alek. This has gone too far."

"How will you help me?" I spoke quietly as I put the scalpel back down on the cart.

"Go to Montreal, Alek. Go to Bean."

"But how? I can't drive a car, can't take public transportation."

"There's something that we used to do as teenagers for fun. It's called train hopping."

"I've read about train hopping, but I thought it was only homeless vagrants that did it for a cheap way to get around."

"If you're careful, you can make it to Montreal without anyone knowing. What you do when you get there is up to you, Alek. I want you to get her back."

Sebastien spoke quickly, explaining the ins and outs of a train yard, how to get onto a car undetected, what safety precautions to take. As he spoke, a million questions arose, poised on the tip of my tongue. Why was Sebastien helping me against his wife's wishes? What would he say to Catherine when she discovered I was gone? Where would I go once I found Bean? I understood then what a difficult position it must have been for him.

Instead, I said, "Thank you."

"I love my daughter, and I love my wife." Sebastien sighed, running his fingers through his thick, dark hair streaked in grey. "Somehow she's become lost in the past few years. I need to find her again."

"Are you talking about your daughter or your wife?"

He paused. "I guess both."

Voices floated in from the hall. Sebastien glanced at the door, then spoke hurriedly. "Catherine is speaking with Dr. Pam down the hall. You don't have much time. Put on Trent's clothes and go down the East stairwell. There is a doorway that opens up at the ground floor where nurses sometimes hide out on break, so the emergency alarm has been deactivated." He turned to leave, then said, "She loves you very much. It's the least I can do for both of you. Keep her safe. Don't try to contact us. I'll find you."

He held out his hand. I took it in my own, and we shook hands.

Sebastien shut the door behind him.

My mind whirling in stunned confusion, joy, fear, I tore off my robe and put on the folded pile of clothes sitting on a chair by Trent's bed. We seemed nearly the same size, and I wondered briefly if this was on purpose. I enfolded the chip in a tissue and placed it the pocket of Trent's jeans. Taking one last look around the room, I walked out the door and down the hallway, hoping to look purposeful. The East stair entrance was only a few metres from the door. I slipped in and walked quickly down the echoing stairwell. The ground floor exit was marked with a sign reading "Emergency Exit Only: Alarm Will Sound." Hoping that Sebastien was right, I pushed on the metal bar. The door swung open silently into an empty alley littered with cigarettes. I noted a lone figure clad in pale green scrubs, but the person didn't look up, intent on sucking the remaining nicotine out of the cigarette as I moved rapidly past and out into the parking lot.

Only after leaving the building did I realize belatedly that it was the first time I had ever shook anyone's hand, person to person. It felt as if Sebastien and I had connected momentarily, two humans acknowledging the other's existence.

The industrialized section of town where I could hop on a train was about four kilometres away. If I walked quickly, I could be there in under an hour. Unfortunately, I felt weak and exhausted from the last few days.

The journey took almost two hours. I guessed that it was very early in the morning. The streets were quiet. Not even the buses were running.

I walked with my hands in my pockets, but my head up, glancing around for any signs of someone coming after me. My heart doubled its beats as a police car cruised by. I must have looked as if I belonged on the streets in the middle of the night, like a shift worker on his way home. The car kept on going.

The houses and storefronts lining the streets I walked began to look older, more faded and rundown. Crude, hastily-drawn graffiti decorated some of the boarded up buildings. Piles of garbage were strewn on the curb. As I walked by one bag that had been ripped open by either a hungry animal or scavenging person, my eye caught the glint of something sparkling in the streetlight. I stopped and nudged the cracked snow globe with my foot; instead of snow, it was filled with sparkling sand and tiny shells swirling slowly in the stirred up water. I smiled, remembering my one experience at a beach.

A few months after my return to the Archambault household, Bean and her friends had decided to celebrate the end of exams by going to Sauble Beach. I had been invited to come along to add swimming to my list of new experiences. Despite the sunny late spring weather, there hadn't been enough warm days to really heat up the water. The beach was nearly empty; I could hear the sounds of seagulls fighting over fish carcasses and the wind blowing across the long dune grasses. Seagulls swooped over our heads where Bean and I sat at a crookedly leaning picnic table, one of its legs sinking in the sand. Shawn chased Kate farther down the beach and tackled her into the surf as she screamed. Russell and Kimber sat on a blanket eating chips and sandwiches and drinking from a thermos.

It was cold. I shivered as I stood up and walked towards the water. I could feel the wet sand sucking up my feet. A wave came up and shocked me. Bean laughed as I stumbled back.

"It's all or nothing," she said, kicking up a little of the surf. "You can't go in slowly. You have to run!"

She grabbed my hand and pulled me towards the water. "Come ON!"

We ran at first, and as the deeper water devoured our legs, we slowed. I gasped with shock as a wave hit my chest, feeling my nerves scream, get out! Cold! Suddenly Bean was on my back, pushing me under the water.

I sucked in a breath just before my mouth and eyes were covered. I opened my eyes, looking around the murkiness. Not much to see here. Bean was under the water too, her cheeks puffed out holding her air, her eyes wide and unfocussed. Her hair floated about her like seaweed, swaying as she moved with the current. My lungs began to protest, so I stood up blowing out stale air and taking in a fresh lungful like a breeching whale.

"You look like a mermaid," I told Bean.

"I don't have a tail," she replied, flicking water at me. I lay back gingerly, hoping the water would hold my weight. I relaxed when I found it would hold me. Somehow it had begun to feel warmer. Back when I had temperature sensors, I registered heat and cold, and it always felt the same; but now, with real skin, I could feel the effects of the cool easing off as I grew accustomed to the water. It didn't feel, so bad—in fact, it felt wonderful!

To touch something is to feel not only the texture and temperature of the object you are touching, but to feel your own skin, how the pads of your fingers give way, how the base of your fingernails pleasantly strum when you scratch an itch; or conversely when touched, how each hair is softly skimmed when someone lays a hand on your arm, how a shivering tingle can radiate through your body from a small point of contact.

But now, my whole body seemed to buzz; my skin, the largest organ, bombarded me with information: the cooling breeze puffing across my arms, the tickling feeling of the hairs on my arms rising with the work of the tiny muscles underneath, making goose bumps to warm the flesh. My face tingled with the spray of water from the waves, then cooled as the water evaporated. I felt the heat of the sun on my closed eyelids, and saw it as a red light projected on a screen.

With my ears just under the water, the teenagers' shrieks mingling with the gulls' own cries were muffled, but I could clearly hear the clicking of pebbles and shells as they were pushed along the bottom by the surging waves.

Being so aware of the different sensations in my body made

me feel very present. I was in love with that moment, completely happy and accepting of where I was now, who I was now; the future seemed as unreachable as the horizon; the past was carried away in the wind.

My mind jumped back to the present as a racoon shuffled from behind a garbage bin, squealing when he saw me. I walked on, spurred by the memory and hope for a future.

20 / AVOIDANCE

A TRAIN WAS rumbling into the yard, brakes squealing as it slowed. I could feel the vehicle rather than hear it. I lay the in darkness of the tall grass just beyond the gravel surrounding the tracks, waiting. Finally, it appeared, car after car smoothly gliding along. It slowed almost imperceptibly; five minutes went by before it came to a complete standstill. Luckily, a boxcar with an open side sat directly in front of me. I stood up cautiously, looking around. The tail of cars continued into the distance; I couldn't see where the train ended. A yard worker was walking in my direction along the tracks bathed in floodlights, inspecting the cars several metres away. He saw me, raised a hand in greeting, and kept walking. I took that as I sign that he didn't mind my presence.

I waited until he came closer, then spoke.

"Where's this train heading?"

The man's lined face was darkly tanned. He looked at me for a moment, pushing his hat back on his head and wiping his forehead.

"This one's going to Halifax. Makes two stops. One in Toronto and one in Montreal."

"How long do you think it'll take to get to Montreal?" I'd read that trains could take days for a trip that would normally take hours by car.

"Not too long. You'd be there by late afternoon."

"Thanks." I held out my hand. The man shook it firmly.

The yard worker continued his inspection down the track. I walked up to the open boxcar and cautiously put a foot on the side, then hoisted myself up. The car was empty except for a pile of what appeared to be old clothing in one corner and a stack of wooden boxes chained to the far end. I wedged myself in.

About half an hour later, the train slowly began accelerating. I could hear nothing of the world outside; only the screeching and rumbling of moving parts, the creaking of the car itself as it swayed from side to side, the rushing and whistling of the wind. I felt too alert, too anxious to fall asleep. I sat uncomfortably, my muscles becoming sore and my skin bruised from the rhythmic jarring. Despite this, my eyelids began to lower until miraculously, I fell asleep.

I awoke to the train whistle. Daylight streamed in through a large crack in the door as I made my way over and sat cross-legged at the edge, my arm tightly wrapped around a side railing. I peered out as the world sped past me. Deer looked up, startled from their grazing in yellow fields. People waved at dirt road crossings and from parks and their own backyards. I wondered how anyone could live in a house that backed onto a train track.

The train began to reduce its speed almost imperceptibly, eventually slowing to a crawl in a busy train yard, which I concluded must be Toronto. I wrenched myself into a standing position. It took me several minutes to fully unfold my stiff body. My joints screamed out and my head ached from the constant noisy vibration. I peered out of a crack between the wall panels. Now that the train had slowed, I could hear a symphony from the massive train yard; voices yelling, engines rumbling, doors clanging shut, trains coupling and uncoupling like teenagers at a darkened house party. I walked the length of the car, jumping up and down a couple of times to loosen my muscles. My stomach felt empty and sore.

I sat and stood up, walked up and down, and did jumping jacks for the next several hours while the train sat in the yard, changing crew and adding cargo. My car was not touched.

Just as the train began its slow acceleration, the door to my car squealed and the crack of daylight widened. A dark figure hopped up, its features obscured by the brilliant backlighting. A second, smaller figure jumped up beside the first and crouched low when it spotted me.

"Looks like we got a cabin-mate, Dini," spoke the smaller figure. By the sound of her voice, I guessed it was a woman. The man pulled the door until it was almost closed. I peered at the two of them, willing my eyes to adjust quickly to the sudden gloom.

'Dini' wore a large, bulky coat that hung past his knees. A dirty, knit hat hid his eyes. Along his left forearm, I could see a large, uneven scar traveling from the wrist to halfway up to the underside of his elbow. It looked like an old wound. The skin was pale pink and puckered. The woman sidled up next to him, rolling up the sleeves of her faded patchwork cloak.

Her left arm also bore a similar scar, although hers seemed more recent. It dawned on me what these scars might be. These were the Invisibles—the rebels, rejects of society—who purposefully removed their Intelli!chips in revolt against what they considered a government who pried too much into their private lives.

"You're awfully crisp lookin' to be takin' a ride like this," the man took a step towards me, fists clenched at his sides. "This here's our car. Got it? You're gonna have to find another one."

"But the train's already started. I can't just—"

"I think he wants us to hold his arms while he takes a step down. Grab him," he instructed the woman. She came towards me, lip curled and shoulders hunched. I backed into a corner far from the door as the man lunged and grabbed me around the arms.

"Let's see if he's got anything worth our time before tossing him." As he held me, his partner shoved her hands roughly into my pockets.

"What's this?" The woman stepped back in surprise, holding the rusty red stained intelli!chip, dried blood flaking off into her hand.

"Hey—why didn't you say you were one of us?" The man loosed his grip on my arms and took the chip, putting it up to his eye as if inspecting it.

"What Magician did you use?"

"What's that?"

The two looked at each other in disbelief.

"Where've you been livin'?" the man said, peering at my face as if reading a map. "A Magician is someone who can turn you Invisible. Get it?"

He handed me back Trent's chip, which I immediately returned to my pocket. I got it. These two thought that I had my implant removed, and that I hired someone to remove it cleanly. It was probably best to let them continue believing that story instead of the less believable truth. I tugged the sleeves further down around my wrists to prevent them from seeing my unblemished skin.

"What d'you call yourself?"

I didn't know what to tell these people. Maybe the truth would be okay. "Alek."

"Alek? Huh. You're gonna have to get a better handle than that. Anyway, I'm Houdini, and this here's Bunny."

"So how long have you two been, uh, Invisible?" I asked.

The woman called Bunny motioned to the corner. We sat down on the cushion of old clothing with our backs against the stack of crates.

"I picked up Bunny after I had gone three years before. She was in a pretty bad way, family kicked her out, she was about to fall off the edge of the planet with all the drugs she was puttin' in her body. I picked her up and cleaned her off."

"He turned me Invisible, else I'd be dead or stuck in some institution somewhere." Bunny said proudly, holding out her scar as if this crude attempt at surgery was a badge of honour. She rummaged around the pockets of her coat until she pulled out a handful of packaged food.

"Granola bar?" she asked. My stomach immediately rumbled in reply. "Say no more," she grinned, and tossed me one of the bars. I tore into it and was finished before the other two had even unwrapped theirs.

"Thank you," I said once I had finished swallowing.

We passed farmlands and small towns, industrialized zones and sparse forests. The crumbling suburbs stood out desolately, with their graffittied strip malls, pyramids of grocery carts towering above the otherwise empty parking lots. Giant houses on tiny strips of land stared out blankly through broken window eyes. Pieces of playground structures lay strewn across overgrown lawns, their skeletons broken or burnt. At one point, we stood by the open door as the train slowed at a crossing. I spotted smoke rising from the chimney of one of the smaller houses in a neat cul-de-sac and slow shadows moving about inside. Between two rusty soccer goal posts, several crops grew, rich and green. The space was crowded with people who were bent over the plants, pulling weeds and watering from cans.

As Houdini and Bunny raised their arms in greeting, I noticed several of the figures wave slowly back. A small girl stood up in the field, clumps of weeds in her fists, and began running towards the train. She was barefoot and wild-looking. From this distance, I could still see her broad smile and flyaway hair, reminding me of Bean as a girl. I raised my hand as she jumped up and down, madly waving both arms at the moving train.

"Is that a town for Invisibles?"

"Yep." Bunny sat down again as the repurposed suburb and its inhabitants vanished behind us. "We call it Scarsboro." I grinned at the name.

"Do you live somewhere in particular?"

"Most of us live in one place or another. When we get itchy for adventure, we leave. Some of us don't stop travellin' ever. Nomadic." I started at the large word coming from Houdini's mouth.

He must have noticed the expression on my face, because he waved a hand and said, "Don't be fooled by us. We're not some dumb, uneducated and unsocialized mucks. Most of us came from somewhere. Somewhere that got to be too much. Too busy, too stressful, too complicated. I grew up in T'ron'o. Went to college. Got a job in a tall building, just like a good Citizen. Hated it."

Bunny nodded in agreement. I noticed that Houdini's rough way of talking began to fade slightly when he spoke of his former life.

"What about you, Bunny? How did you end up an Invisible?" Bunny sighed and shifted in her nest of jackets.

"I didn't have it so easy. Like lots of Citizens, my parents were given a loan they couldn't afford by a bank that had more money than it knew what t'do with. When they lost their jobs, just like everyone else during the Petroleum Parade, the bank took back the house. What's a bank need with a house, anyways? We lived in a car for a bit, but that gets pretty tired, 'specially when stuff like schools ask you for your address. You can't very well say you live in a Toyota Bolt at the corner of Hooper and Staynor. When I was fifteen, I took off and made it into the same town of Invisibles that Houdini ended up. Felt pretty much invisible for years before that anyways. The folks took care of me there. Taught me how to live outside of regular society."

"And how 'bout you, Alek?" Dini squinted at me through the

shadows. "You seem young to be on your own. How old are you, anyways?"

I stopped at the thought. How old am I? My chronological age, since I was activated, was six years, but parts of me were even newer. Obviously, I couldn't tell them I was six. How old was I?

I was young; I was old. My body was as new as an infant's but it had the size and maturity of a young adult. Though I had the knowledge of an elder, I had so much to learn. In many ways, I was naive. I had experienced a thousand lives and hardly begun living my one life. In this way, Bean and I were alike. She'd always struggled, not acting the age people expected of her.

"I'm eighteen," I decided. It was an age on the abyss. Not quite adult, no longer child. Sometimes wise, often times foolish. I seemed to estimate accurately, because neither of them looked surprised.

"Where ya headed?" 'Dini said, scratching his full beard.

"Montreal."

"What's in Montreal? Wait, let me guess: a girl?" I smiled in spite of myself.

"Yup, it's a girl all right, look at that dopey grin!"

"What's her name?" Bunny smiled, showing crooked, yet surprisingly clean teeth.

"Bean. Sabine." I think of her hair, her eyes, her smile, a jumble of memories that I had slipped into my back pocket, always there.

"She know you're comin'?"

"Yes, I mean, I think so. She sent me a message about where she is."

"How'd you two meet?" Bunny rested her elbow on a propped

knee and her chin on her elbow. She looked at me with interest, reminding me of a talk show host.

"Uh, I worked for her parents." Houdini nodded in understanding.

"Yep. Say no more. Two young paramours from different classes, forbidden love: you're a regular Romeo n' Juliet."

"You have no idea how different," I said, grinning. Despite the alarming first reception, I was warming up to these two.

"She runnin' away with you? Gettin' rid of her tracker?"
I paused. What were our plans? I couldn't very well be seen in public with her. Suddenly my running away seemed like an absurd idea. I slumped against the side of the car.

"Hey, hey . . ." Bunny put an arm on my shoulder. "It's gonna be okay. You need us to help? Go see her first?"

"Wha . . . why would you do that for me?" Bunny and Houdini looked at one another.

"We like you." Bunny smiled. "That's all there is to it."

"Besides," Houdini added. "One less tracker on this planet is one step closer to a free world."

I wanted to tell them everything. The whole story. Who I used to be, my transformation who I'd become. I took a deep breath.

"I can't have you going out of your way for me until you know the whole story. I'm not exactly what you think I am. I never had a chip in my life until yesterday."

As I began talking, Bunny and Houdini remained perfectly still and silent. They watched me, listening with their mouths slightly open. The deeper into my story I got, the easier it became to tell. The words came out of me in a rush, desperate to be heard.

When I was finished, I felt exhausted, exhilarated, but very nervous. My travelling companions had yet to say a word to me.

"Well, that's just about the most amazin' thing I've ever heard," Houdini finally said after several moments.

"So you're tryin' to fit in to the very society we're runnin' from," Bunny said.

"I don't know what I'm trying to do. All I know is that I need to find Bean again. I need to see her. I can't be without her." The two paused again, quietly reflecting.

"Any misfit of society is welcome with us," Houdini said, "but you might want to get rid of that tracker."

"What do you mean?"

"You don't have to use the tracker for them to find you. They can track you by satellite, find you anytime, anywhere."

"What do I do, then?" I felt a sudden panic, as if TARIA could see me and hear everything.

"Toss it."

I took Trent's chip out of my pocket. I could barely feel it in my palm, it was so thin and light. I walked over to the open door of the car and held my arm out. The wind instantly whipped it out of my hand; I watched the speck flash briefly across the side of the train before it was sucked under and disappeared.

Houdini grinned, closing the door.

"Like magic."

21 / ARTISTRY

A heart is not judged by how much you love; but
by how much you are loved by others.
– L. Frank Baum, *The Wonderful Wizard of Oz*

"WON'T BE LONG now," Houdini spoke through a mouthful as we shared lunch, a couple of apples that he had sliced with an ancient-looking, but well-cared for Swiss Army knife.

"I'd recommend jumping off when the train stops at Montreal-Ouest. It's a busy place. Lots of people, but lots of distractions. Watch out for the bulls, though; that's railyard security."

"Thanks for the advice. I have a map that should help me find where I'm going."

"What're you gonna do about tonight? The streets aren't the place for you."

"I don't know. I'll find somewhere . . . "

Bunny looked quickly to Houdini, who raised his eyebrows. She turned again to me.

"We're coming with you."

"That's very kind of you, but I'll be okay."

"You need us. You haven't been walking this earth long enough to know what's what."

"You don't know what I know," I began, "I have more knowledge stored in this brain than—"

"Garbage," Houdini interrupted. "You have the curious and stunned expression of a newborn baby. You'll be a walking target. You need us. We know a place where you can stay for a night. It's settled."

"It's good to have friends," Bunny said softly. I reached out to squeeze her hand. Besides Bean, I'd never had real friends before.

Just as Houdini predicted, our train slowed at a track switch to let a passenger train pass from the other direction. We hopped off the train just before it reached the yard. The place was quiet and empty except for a few lone cars. I kept waiting to hear someone shout at us as we stepped across the tracks and climbed over the chain-linked fence.

As we walked away from the yard, I started thinking about TARIA. They weren't simply going to let me walk away from them. Catherine had a lot invested in my life. Was I being naive to think it would be easy just simply to leave, that no one would be looking for me? I was wearing Trent's clothing and had cut out his Intelli!chip.

"You look uneasy," Bunny spoke as our legs swished through long grass. We could now hear cars in the distance; we were close to a road. "What's goin' on in that head of yours?"

"I can't just walk around a city and expect that no one will notice. Someone must be coming after me. I'm too important for their research. I am their research," I added.

Houdini removed his knit hat and long coat. Handing both items to me, he said, "Put these on. They won't expect you've got friends helping out."

I removed Trent's jacket and left it on the ground. I pulled Houdini's hat far down over my head and put on his coat, feeling better.

We walked for hours through the city. Houdini and Bunny seemed to know exactly where they were going. For two people who shunned society, they knew the city inside and out.

As the sun hid behind the tall buildings, I began to slow down, exhausted and hungry. I didn't want to ask them to stop, since neither of my travelling companions seemed ready to rest.

Finally, they stopped in front of a tattoo studio. An artistically rendered sign hanging above the doorway read, "Dermatic Arts."

"We're here," announced Houdini.

"We're staying here?"

"A friend of ours." Bunny said. "He's a good guy, for someone who still lives with Citizens."

As we walked through the door, I was amazed at the diversity of the clientele. An older woman, maybe in her 60s, sat in a chair beside the reception desk, quietly reading a paperback. She wore a long flowing skirt and a cardigan. She wasn't wearing makeup and didn't have any obvious markings or piercings. She didn't look nervous. I thought maybe she was waiting for someone. We sat down beside two young men in their early twenties, who were flipping though a binder of tattoo art; apparently their choice of permanent body art had been a last minute decision. The woman dressed in a business suit sitting across from us had more metal on her face than I had as a machine.

When the receptionist behind the desk, who had so many tattoos on her bare arms that they look like sleeves, called out, "Moira," the older woman closed her book and stood.

"Back for more, are we?" the receptionist smiled at her.

"Just one more," said the woman.

"I've heard that one before."

I caught a flash of something black with bared teeth curling around her ankle as she walked into the next room. When the receptionist looked over to us, frowning slightly, Houdini stood.

"May I help you?"

"Houdini and Bunny here to see Nook."

"Do you have an appointment?"

"No. If you would be so kind as to tell him we're here, I'm sure he'll see us."

The receptionist stared at us for a few moments more, then got up and went into a back room.

Large binders sat at the table to my left. I picked one up and leafed through the pictures: birds, reptiles, and animals, Celtic swirls, Asian symbols, and barcodes. A design detailed with entangled black lines caught my eye and I stopped at the page.

"Nook will see you." The receptionist with the permanent sleeves had returned, looking friendlier. She motioned for us to follow her.

We walked into what seemed to be a break room. A small table and four chairs sat in the middle. To the left, a counter with a sink and cupboards took up one wall. A fridge stood against another. The walls were bare.

"Dini, how are you doing, you old fraud? And Bunny! Still hopping trains with this guy, huh?"

A large man with a long, braided beard entered the room through another door, strode over us and enveloped Bunny and Houdini in a huge hug. Unlike the receptionist, he had only an intricate band around one forearm and a long lizard snaking its way up the other arm. His face had no piercings other than a wide disk in each ear, which had stretched his lobes so that they almost touched his wide shoulders.

"This here's Alek. He needs a place to stay for a night." Nook took two large strides over and shook my hand firmly in his large, hearty grasp.

"Nice to meet you, Alek. Any friend of these two," he said, scrutinizing me, my face, my arms, my legs.

"Hungry?" We all nodded vehemently. Nook looked over to the receptionist. "Suze, I'm taking lunch for the next hour."

"Got it." Suze nodded to us, smiling slightly as she returned to the waiting room, closing the door behind her.

"Please sit," Nook said to us and motioned to the chairs. We removed our hats and coats, placing them on a coat rack in the corner. I eased myself into a chair, feeling painfully exhausted. I felt tense energy draining from my body.

Nook turned to the fridge and took out various packages of meats and cheeses, fresh vegetables, and condiments. As he pulled a large loaf of fresh bread out of the cupboard, he asked, "So Alek, where are you headed?"

I gave him the address to the school of music Bean was attending.

"That's not far from here. About twenty minutes' walk." He cut large slabs from the bread and folded large slices of meat on top. "What brings you to Montreal?"

"He's following a girl," Bunny said, as if it explained everything.

Nook nodded knowingly. For the next several minutes, we sat silently—except for the rumbling of our stomachs—while Nook prepared the food. Finally he turned from the counter and joined us at the table, placing in the centre a tray of sandwiches piled high. The mound was surrounded by a colourful array of pickles and neatly sliced vegetables.

"Apparently skin inking is only one of your artistic skills," I said, indicating the tray.

"Thanks," Nook said. "Tastes even better than it looks. Dig in."

We didn't need to be asked twice. Bunny, Houdini, and I all reached for the pile of food at once, each grabbing a different sandwich. Nook opened the fridge and took out several cans of Coke, placing them on the table.

"Oooh," Houdini muttered to his sandwich before biting into it. "Nothin' like Montreal smoked meat." I murmured an enthusiastic reply, my mouth already full. We ate steadily in silence.

Half an hour later, I was tipped back slightly on my chair, my stomach sticking out slightly. I had never felt so full.

"Thank you," I said. "That was amazing."

Nook smiled at me. "My pleasure. You look like you needed a half-decent meal." He began clearing dishes. Houdini groaned as he rose from the table to help clean up and Bunny joined him. She began to fill the sink with soapy water to wash the dishes. I began to rise, but she motioned to me to sit.

"Why do you still live in the city?" I asked Nook as he bustled around the small room.

"I may live here, but I'm still Invisible," he said. He leaned toward me and held out his arm. His intricate tattoo covered a scar where the Intelli!chip should have been.

"This city has always been my home. I'm a go-between for people like you who aren't sure where they fit in anymore. Not everyone can leave society the way Bunny and Houdini have. You have to do what's right for you."

Bunny unexpectedly made a small squeak. She pointed at the Intelli!net on the wall. We all turned to see my face taking up the left side of the screen; it looked like a mug shot without the prisoner ID number at the bottom. The right side scrolled through my height, weight, clothing I was presumed to be wearing, the fact that I may have been headed for Montreal. I read the scrolling text, feeling light-headed. It described me as a former employee of TARIA who had disappeared with valuable information that belonged to the company. I was deemed possibly dangerous. They had hidden the truth with a more acceptable version. I guess TARIA didn't agree that I was solely Catherine's intellectual property. If word got out that TARIA had lost its most state-of-the-art, wildly unpredictable, and morally questionable experiment, the company's stocks would plummet, and they'd go bankrupt. A hollow laugh escaped me. Nook swiftly walked over to the !screen and shut it off with a sweep of his fingers.

"Guess you're more important than you thought," Bunny said to me, placing a hand on my arm.

"You okay with that?" Houdini turned to Nook. "Harbouring a fugitive an' all?"

"Any friend of yours," Nook replied for the second time that afternoon, surveying me. "Somehow I don't think that's the truth, or the whole of it, anyway."

"Right now I just want to find Bean. Then we'll figure things out."

"Well, I can help you get to her by the safest route possible. Is there anything else I can do for you?" Nook asked.

"Pack me up some of those sandwiches for later," Bunny said over her shoulder. Houdini mumbled his agreement.

I had something else in mind since the moment I walked in. It might have seemed like a strange request, given my situation. I took a breath.

"I want a tattoo."

"Really?" Bunny looked surprised.

"Why not, we're gonna be here for a few hours," Houdini said, looking over to Nook.

"Fell in love with my art, did you?" Nook smiled. "It happens."

He opened the door to reception and called out, "Suze? Can I see the ink sampler for a moment please?"

Suze brought in the binder that I had looked through in the waiting room. I knew exactly what I wanted since I had made the decision after seeing it in the waiting area. I opened the binder to the page and showed him the image.

"Sure thing. Where?" I pointed to a spot on my chest.

Nook took me into an adjoining room and motioned for me to sit in a black reclining chair. I felt as though I was back in the hospital. The room was very clean, containing a spotless sink and counter with various instruments lying carefully on it in sealed packages. A plastic tub sat under the counter for biohazardous materials: used needles, cotton pads, and bandages.

As he pressed an inked outline on my skin for tracing, he said, "So how'd you get mixed up with those two? I have a feeling it's quite the story."

"I. . . I don't know where to begin." I suddenly felt the weight of my existence pressing down.

"Begin at the beginning."

The weight of my secret, my uncertain past, my undetermined future, settled upon me, and I couldn't speak.

Nook must have sensed the sheer exhaustion that I felt, so he said, "Tell you what: I'll give you an Intelli!pad, so you can write it all down. You look like you need to get this off your chest, but I know the feeling like you just can't gather the energy to do it out loud. And I get the feeling that this is one story that needs to be passed on for the record, for the future to look back on."

Nook continued to work methodically, both of us in silence. The actual tattooing process hurt like a thousand needle-pricks would, but nothing like the agony of having my entire body replaced.

My mind drifted away from the pain. What was I doing with this new life? For how long would I be free until my makers caught up with me? I knew without a doubt that not a single moment of this strange existence meant a thing if Bean wasn't in it. I felt an intense physical pain that was not from the needles piercing my skin but at the thought of living without her.

"Done," Nook spoke finally, taking a final wipe across the tattoo. Blood seeped from the black lines and the surrounding skin appeared red and inflamed. He held up a mirror, and I couldn't help but smile at the mark that had been made on my body. I played the words over slowly in my mind: My. Body. Nook taped gauze over the tattoo. I thought only of Bean as

I half heard him instructing me how to keep it clean while it healed. As he led me back into the lounge, he handed me the Intelli!pad.

"No hurry. You have all night. If you need to sleep, there's a pullout bed in the other room over there and some blankets in the cupboard." He motioned to a couch in the corner. Gently closing the door behind him, he left the room.

22 / ACCEPTANCE

FOR THE SECOND time that day and the second time in my life, I find myself recounting the story of my existence for another stranger-turned-friend. This time, in writing, using as much detail as I can recall: as you said, for the record, for posterity. I feel as though I've returned to my pre-biological self; I am drained of all emotion as I type out my story. My fingers ache, but my head is strangely light. I don't know how this ending will play out, but I know wherever it takes me, Bean will be there. Nothing else matters.

I write. I eat more of the leftover sandwiches and drink water. I rise and stretch. I get back to writing. I stand up and go to the bathroom. I write again. I pace the room. I write until I can't write anymore, since the future has yet to be written. I put the Intelli!pad down on the counter.

I sleep and I sleep.

I awaken to low murmuring voices and the hum of a tattoo needle coming from the other room. My chest aches where my own tattoo is now permanently etched. I groggily shuffle over to the counter and open a drawer. Rifling through it, I find fresh bandages. I carefully peel off the old one covering my tattoo and replace it with a clean one.

The door opens, and Dini and Bunny enter.

"Good, you're up! We were beginning to worry," Bunny hugs me, then pulls away as she notices me wince.

"Tattoo," I explain, pointing to my chest. "What time is it?"

"Almost seven . . . at night" Dini adds. "You've slept a whole night and a day. I'm guessing you didn't have the most restful night on the train. Hungry?" As he speaks, he opens up the fridge and pulls out a container.

"Nook made breakfast, but we saved you some."

He warms up the leftover hash browns and the omelette filled with red peppers, onions, and ham. I pick at my food, nervous about what lies ahead of me.

Finally, it is time for me to go. Nook has given me directions on how to get to the music school. We stand in the doorway leading to a back alley. I am wearing a clean blue t-shirt that Nook has given me, along with the jeans—now freshly washed—and the pair of shoes that I had taken from Trent. Houdini's overcoat is draped over my arm. I hold it out to him, but he shakes his head.

"Keep it for now. We'll cross paths again someday. You know you'll always find a friend with the Invisibles. Just tell them you know me." He shakes my hand solemnly. Bunny stifles a sob and squeezes me hard.

"Good luck."

I put on the coat and walk out into the crisp night air. In the dark alley, the droning of car engines and the echoing of laughter drift on the air. The shadows swallow me up, and I'm swept away with the city's sounds.

I walk, keeping my head low, looking up only occasionally to check the street signs. Groups of people pass me, going to a show, coming from dinner, chatting and smiling with ease. I envy the way they can take every breath, every step, for granted.

Finally, I reach the performance hall of the music school. A sign advertises the concert performance by exceptional students. I stand briefly in front of it, observing the people who walk in. They are greeted briefly at the door, but no one is collecting tickets or charging admission. I follow a group through the doors and into the building.

"There is still room at the back, but take your seats quietly please," an usher informs us. "The concert has already begun."

As I walk into the music hall, I hear her before I see her. The cello's sounds curl around the air, weaving in and out of the other music. As I stand at the back, protected in the dark, I see her on stage. She cradles the cello in her hands and hugs it between her knees like she's protecting it from the world, her left arm wrapped loosely around it, the neck held between her fingers. Her head is down, not reading the music, because after a few scans of a piece she's always had it down by heart. No, her head is down and slightly tilted as if trying to hear a sound emanating from further away than right beside her ear. Her long graceful fingers pluck and her bow carves or caresses the strings, depending on the mood of the music. She is completely out of the world when she plays, or maybe the opposite: she is so staunchly in the present moment, that it is impossible to distract her. I wish I felt like that. I wish something consumed me so wholly that I became that thing. That's exactly how I feel when I'm with her: nothing else matters but the moment we're in. I'm not thinking about whether I'll ever be free, or if I'll ever pass for normal or whether anyone will ever accept me for who I am.

I am in the hall surrounded by a few hundred people, and they are all shadows compared to the person up on that stage. She is in the spotlight, but that's the way I always see her. I want to climb up to her and lay my head on her lap and . . . I experience an odd sensation, like a part of me is up there with her. I can feel the energy emanating from the audience, these waves of support; but I'm also part of the crowd enjoying the experience and feeling the love Bean is pouring into her music. We are all sharing this one moment, and Bean is leading the experience. And I feel glad to know her. No. Not glad. Proud. I am proud to be with her.

All the fights that she's had with her parents over the years, all the discouragement she's felt, it all melts away. I can see it in the expression on her face. Despite her concentration, her face is more relaxed than ever. Her mouth is half open in what seems like a private smile, even with the large crowd focusing in on her. Her eyes, sparkling under the bright stage lights, reflect complete joy. There's only Bean and her music. This is exactly where she is meant to be, and it's astonishingly beautiful. I want a purpose like that in my life; but then I realize that I've got it all wrong.

My whole life is the purpose.

I tear my eyes away from Bean and look around me. It is dark, but I can sense people surrounding me. I am aware of our collective breath as we all witness the same moment. It's as if I can feel every person sitting in the music hall, walking outside, driving on the highways, falling asleep in their homes.

Images rush through my mind. Bean's face shaped like a heart. Bean's long hair like a river down her back. My face buried in her hair, my body lying against the curve of her spine. Bean laughing with crinkled eyes and mouth wide, surprised. Bean at age twelve. Bean now. Bean's soft hands and mouth. The way she walks in my dreams.

The music has stopped. There is a burst of applause, which carries the audience's love and appreciation in waves to the front of the stage. Bean stands and bows slightly, her eyes scan the crowds, squinting, frowning. I tentatively put a hand up in the air, wondering if she can see me through the lights, through this strange clothing that hides me. The applause dies down as Bean exits somewhere behind the curtains in the wings. I put my arm down slowly, and it takes me a moment to notice that I've been holding my breath. The stage lights fade as the house lights come on dimly, and then Bean is there in the flesh, in front of me. Her eyes see me, as they've always seen me. I gather her up in my arms like a ball of unravelled wool, and she leans into me, not caring about the other people in the room. On the skin of my face, I feel puffs of air from her mouth. I feel her breath catch in anticipation. Her lips touch mine with a million tiny electric jolts—no pain, just softness and warmth. Something begins happening in my torso, in my heart. She is warm and smooth and real. We hold each other and kiss and kiss as if it was the most natural thing in the world; and it is.

Her hands travel over my back and move around to my chest.

I flinch as she brushes over the new wound.

"What's wrong?"

"Nothing, I just had one last change. An upgrade." Bean raises one beautiful eyebrow.

I unbutton the top of my shirt, pull the fabric aside on my left side, and lift up the corners of the bandage covering the tattoo. It's bloody and oozing, but the outline is there. The hand is drawn in black, swirling lines. The swirls condense at the fingertips, almost like fingerprints. It is open and resting on my chest, over my heart. It is a reminder of my humanity. Love, warmth, creativity: all the blessings I've been given wrapped within bone and tissue.

"It's beautiful," she breathes, placing her own hand on top of my new one, not quite touching. The heat of her hand hovering close to my skin penetrates deep into my chest, mirroring the warmth emanating from my own body. She leans in, with one hand still over my chest and tenderly kisses a spot just above the fresh wound.

"*Sawubona,*" she speaks softly.

"*Ngikhona,*" I answer.

Her free hand finds my own.

/ EPILOGUE

THE COUPLE WALKING hand in hand move through the crowded nighttime streets. They glide past groups of young people walking and talking animatedly on the sidewalks, eating and laughing, bundled up warmly under patio heaters. No one takes any notice of the young woman with the wild hair and the cello case slung across her shoulder or the young man with dark hair and wide, searching eyes, collar turned up on his worn overcoat. They walk with purpose, with a sense of destination. As they stop at a pedestrian crossing, the young man wraps his arms around the young woman. She looks up and smiles at him. No one stops and stares. Why would they?

Although they stand at the curb, they don't appear to be waiting for the light to change. They are standing, taking in the moment, aware of their surroundings, of each other. The young man stares up at the sky as if looking for the few stars bright enough to shine though the flood of city lights. He squeezes her tightly and murmurs something in her ear. She closes her eyes and leans into him.

"Where do we go from here?" she whispers.

"I know a place," he answers.

For the briefest of moments, he glances past her, a furtive look so fleeting that one might have failed to notice it.

Yet those who follow them like shadows skulking in the alleyways don't miss a thing.

The light turns and they walk on.

/ TO THE READER

YOU'VE MADE IT! Thank you for following this story to the end. If you loved reading this book as much as I did writing it, please take a moment to spread the word through social media and write a review at your favourite online retailer or book review site.

Keep in touch to learn more about *Invisibles*, the upcoming 2016 sequel to *Being Human*.

Thanks!
Christina Grant, Author

twitter.com/@cgrantwriter
facebook.com/cgrantwriter
smashwords.com/profile/view/CGrantWriter

Being Human is available to purchase in electronic form.
Order it today from your favourite online retailer.

/ ACKNOWLEDGEMENTS

Thank you...and you...and you...

To the librarians and baristas for helping to make the libraries and cafés my homes away from home—the quiet spaces, amazing views and delicious cappuccinos — especially The Ideas Exchange and the Melville Café in downtown Galt, Ontario.

To my friends and colleagues who read the earlier unfinished drafts, and encouraged me to continue anyway.

To my student readers who gave me such glowing, positive feedback and who were almost as impatient as I was see the book in print.

To Kim, who gave me the book that inspired this whole journey.

To Alana—who probably read the story even more times than I did—whose insights were spot-on, whose praise lifted me up, and whose critique motivated me to write better.

To my parents and parents in-law, who gave me the invaluable gift of time.

To my boys, who let me be somebody other than Mom for a while.

To my sister, Kathy: we will always be each other's biggest fans! Your cover was perfect, and more than I could have imagined. And I am beyond grateful for your artistic eye for the print version layout.

To my husband, Neil, who always told me that I could write a novel and gave me the time and space and love to do it.

And to the grandparents I never had the opportunity to get to know. I hope I've inherited your creativity, ingenuity, quirkiness, and humour.

/ ABOUT THE AUTHOR

Christina Grant is a reader, writer, and lover of all things bookish. When she doesn't have her eyes locked on the latest book (her own or someone else's), she's spending as much time as possible in, on, and around Georgian Bay with her husband, their two sons, and their dog. She is also an elementary teacher-librarian who shares her love of words with her many enthusiastic students.

She's a terrible dancer but swears she was one in another life.

Made in the USA
Charleston, SC
18 March 2015